The Big Snapper

Katherine Holubitsky

Orca Book Publishers

Library and Archives Canada Cataloguing in Publication
Holubitsky, Katherine
The big snapper / Katherine Holubitsky.

(Orca young readers)
ISBN 10: 1-55143-563-2 / ISBN 13: 978-1-55143-563-3

I. Title. II. Series.

PS8565.O645B53 2006 jC813'.54 C2006-903447-8

First published in the United States, 2006
Library of Congress Control Number: 2006928963

Summary: Eddie loves fishing with Granddad and listening to his tall tales, but when his grandfather becomes seriously ill, Eddie must find ways to cope with the changes in his world.

Free teachers' guide available: www.orcabook.com

Orca Book Publishers gratefully acknowledges the support for its publishing programs provided by the following agencies: the Government of Canada through the Book Publishing Industry Development Program and the Canada Council for the Arts, and the Province of British Columbia through the BC Arts Council and the Book Publishing Tax Credit.

Typesetting and cover design by Doug McCaffry
Cover & interior illustrations by Samia Drisdelle

Orca Book Publishers
PO Box 5626 Stn B
Victoria, BC Canada
V8R 6S4

Orca Book Publishers
PO Box 468
Custer, WA USA
98240-0468

www.orcabook.com
Printed and bound in Canada.
Printed on 100% PCW recycled paper.
010 09 08 07 • 5 4 3 2

For baby Sophia

And in memory of Myron Holubitsky,

a much loved grandfather

Chapter 1

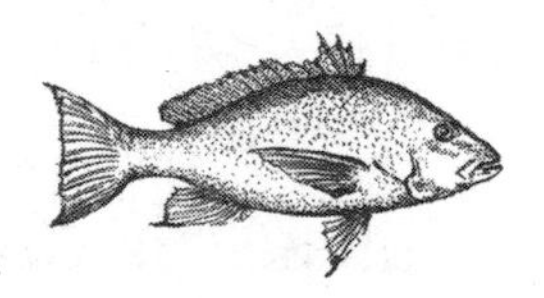

Eddie peers through the mist toward the rocky shore. He watches to see how long it will take to lose sight of Granddad's cabin. The small gray building disappears in and out of the fog, becoming smaller and smaller. Finally it fades into the larger outline of towering cedars and is gone.

Granddad winks from where he sits with his hand on the throttle of the engine. He steers the small skiff farther out into the dark waters of the bay. Eddie turns to feel the moist breeze on his face as they head out to sea.

The bow bounces in the wake of a sleek white yacht, causing the hull of the old skiff to shudder. They pass a large fishing vessel with many rods fixed to the side.

Eddie runs his hand along the weather-beaten gunwale. He shuffles his gumboots, leaving scuff marks in the dent in the bow beneath his feet. "Granddad," he calls above the sound of the skiff's engine. "You've never told me about the first time you saw the big snapper."

"The very first time?" Granddad repeats loudly.

Eddie nods. He watches as Granddad considers the pattern of the water. He watches him judge the distance they are from shore. They have reached one of their favorite fishing spots. Granddad cuts the engine. "Well, perhaps I haven't," he says. He lets the long anchor chain rumble out.

Eddie fishes in a bucket of water for a chunk of octopus while Granddad prepares the line. He knows he'll hear the story as soon as the line is out. When he is ready, Granddad motions that it is time for Eddie to fix the bait onto the hook. Granddad's hands are shaky, so for more than a year the job of baiting the hook has fallen to Eddie.

Sure enough, with the chunk of octopus well on its way to the bottom of the bay, Granddad settles in to tell his story.

"The first time I ran into that old snapper," he begins, "I was eighteen years old. I was a strapping young fellow back then with hair as black as a raven, and I stood just over seven feet tall."

Eddie is clearly amazed. Granddad stands only a little taller than himself now, and he's just over five feet. He'd been measured at school. But he also knows better than to interrupt the story.

"It was on a day much like today," Granddad continues. "In fact I was sitting right about in this very same spot. I was out in this skiff, which was brand spanking new at the time. I'd bought it with the first money I'd made working at the cannery, and I was mighty proud of it. Not five minutes after I'd dropped my line, the bait was nabbed and my line started peeling off at a terrific rate. I cranked down on the drag, but that didn't do any good. It was running real low, so I cranked down all the way, leaned back and put all I had into it."

Granddad pauses to open the lunch basket and pour coffee from a thermos. He leans forward. The steam rising from the mug is swallowed by the mist in the air. "Well, that fish had taken every inch of my line when the boat suddenly lurched forward. The next thing I knew I was skimming across the water at a mind-boggling speed. In no time at all we'd left the bay."

"Why didn't you cut the line?"

"That would have made sense. But when the boat lurched forward, I was slammed into the floor and I couldn't move. From then on the force of the wind and the speed we were going kept me there. We traveled south, passing the ferry from the mainland. We overtook a couple of speedboats moving at a pretty good clip. I could see the Coast Guard cutter up ahead. Within a few seconds it was also in our wake." Granddad chuckles. "If only I could have seen the look on the captain's face. I imagine he was some surprised. Everything was passing in a blur, when suddenly I spotted a streak of orange above the waves."

"Was it the snapper?"

Granddad nods. "It was the snapper. The biggest and strongest red snapper I'd ever seen."

Eddie's eyes widen. "How big?"

"Well, let's see." Granddad considers Eddie. "Maybe about the length of you plus half again, but more the weight of a grizzly bear. Back then the water was cleaner, and there weren't so many commercial boats. The fish had a better chance to get real big. He was a young buck. He had to be to have that much strength. I have to admit, I was impressed. After breaking the surface, he made a perfect arch over a fellow in a kayak. But before he disappeared beneath the waves again, he turned and cursed me with a shiny black eye."

"Were you scared?"

"Sure I was scared. But I didn't have time to think. We were still moving along at close to the speed of sound. I knew we'd long passed Moresby Island—I'd seen the totems of Ninstints. We flew past the Sunshine Coast and a parade of coastal towns. The land changed and I had an idea we were skirting the coast of Oregon. But I had little time to think because when I turned forward again, a giant rock rose from the waves. I realized I was headed straight for it. For the second time, the big snapper rose above the surface. This time he grinned, showing me two rows of terrible teeth—between them was the end of my line. He gave one last yank, let go, veered starboard and dove. But I continued along the path he'd set me on. I crashed head-on into the island of Alcatraz."

Granddad motions toward Eddie's feet. "That's how my skiff got that big dent you've got your boots resting in. But if it wasn't for the rock that stopped me, who knows how the ride would have come to an end? As it was, the jolt sent me out of the boat like an arrow. Being seven feet tall you can imagine what a projectile I made. I soared over a high wall and landed on a trampoline."

"A trampoline?"

Granddad nods. "It was right in the middle of the exercise yard of the prison on Alcatraz. I was surrounded by the most notorious and dangerous criminals in all of the United States. Thick-chested—because they didn't have much else to do but exercise—hairy guys with tattoos of spiders on their cheeks and no teeth. I stepped from the trampoline and shook myself off. The prisoners fell silent a moment and stared up at me. You have to remember that I was skinnier than every one of those crooks and murderers, but I was also seven feet tall. Suddenly the ugliest one of them stepped forward. A long wormy scar stood from his bald head, and he was missing half an ear. Grabbing me roughly,

he hauled me forward. 'This one,' he hollered, holding my arm in the air, 'is on our team.'

"It seemed the fellows were in the middle of choosing teams for a basketball game. I guess he decided I'd make a good center. I was in no position to say no, so I took my place on his team. I could feel the eyes of the captain of the other team on my back as I crossed the yard. When I turned he slammed a fist against the concrete wall and glowered at me. I swallowed hard.

"The game didn't last very long. There was a referee, but he was knocked out for calling a penalty in the first minute. Everything went downhill from there. There were fouls for holding, scratching, hair-pulling and wedgie-giving. But no one to call them. Breakaways ended in pileups, and the point guards were held in headlocks if they tried to make a play. I worked hard though, despite facing a crowd of angry mugs every time I headed down the court. I'd learned from my granddad to try my best no matter how strange the circumstances seemed.

"It was ten to nothing for us. I'd scored all but two points when I was set up for another dunk. I had the ball. All at once the defense on the other team rushed me. Grabbing me around the knees and chest, they swept me off my feet. The captain counted to three and they heave-hoed. I flew into the air, leaving that yard the same way as I'd come in. It was a good thing those fellows were strong, because they pitched me a long way. I landed in San Francisco Bay. Spotting my boat on the rocks, I swam back to it.

"There wasn't much damage other than that big dent. It proved to still be seaworthy, so I started the engine and headed for home."

"Wow," says Eddie when he realizes Granddad is finished his story. "And that was the first time you saw him?"

"The very first time. Now, look here, Eddie. We've got something." Granddad tests the line. "You get the gaff ready in case it's one of those hundred pound halibuts like we caught last year."

Chapter 2

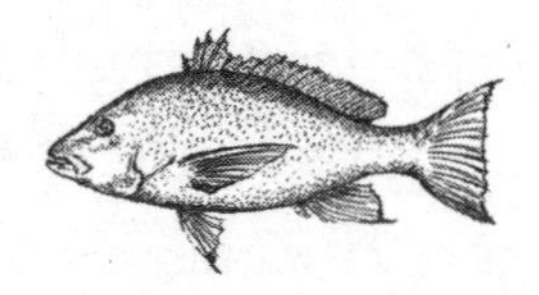

It's late afternoon when Eddie and Granddad start toward the wharf with four rock cod in their basket. Eddie wishes there were more. He knows his mother will say it's barely enough to feed the family, let alone leave any extra to sell to the cannery.

Eddie's gaze wanders across the gray sea. He watches a flock of cormorants bob on the waves, but he is also always on the lookout for the big snapper. If they could catch the big snapper—well, that would change things for sure! Grandma could buy new glasses so she didn't trip over things, and Mom could buy a vacuum cleaner to replace her worn-out broom. And maybe if there was enough left over Eddie could buy his own bike instead of sharing the beat-up old thing he'd found in the dump with his friend, Jake. Eddie's eyes settle on a spot, which, as he watches, becomes the ferry from the mainland.

Eddie has never been to the mainland. It's hundreds of miles away from Haida Gwaii, or the Queen Charlotte Islands, where he lives. In the summer, the ferry brings tourists from Prince Rupert to Graham Island, which is the largest of the islands. Wearing shorts and sun hats, they spill from the belly of the boat in their trucks and campers. They clamber across the beaches and roar about in speedboats, startling the bald eagles that perch in the gnarled arbutus trees on shore. They fill the village with chatter as they walk up and down the dirt road, looking for things to buy.

Granddad tells Eddie that the tourists bring money to the island. This may be so, but Eddie has always preferred their home in the winter. This is when the winds howl through Hecate Strait, whipping the chop to dangerous heights, and the ferry sometimes does not run at all. Eddie and Granddad and all those who live year-round on the island have the beaches and the fish to themselves.

Seagulls circle above the skiff, screaming for the fish Eddie has caught. He leaps to the wharf and secures the boat. He helps Granddad to his feet then carries the tackle and baskets to the house. Granddad has difficulty walking—he shuffles slowly, like something's holding him back. "Some days it feels like the anchor's got tangled around my ankle," he'd once told Eddie. "But when I look down there's nothing there."

Much to Eddie's surprise, Mom is not interested in their catch. She is rearranging the cabin. She has come up with a plan.

"We are going to invite tourists to stay with us," she tells them. "Eddie, they will stay in your room. You will bunk with Granddad and Grandma will sleep with me. It's what the tourists call a bed and breakfast. Now, I want you to clear your desk and move all your books into Granddad's room. I need a space to serve breakfast to our guests. We don't have much but we want to make them comfortable. And don't look so glum, it's only for the summer."

Eddie does as he's told. He and Granddad eat the supper Grandma has prepared while his mother continues to fuss in his room. She carries his clam-digging shovel and his specially crafted rock-turning stick to Granddad's room. She replaces the curtains Grandma had sewn from sheets, with lacey store-bought ones. "An expense we can hardly afford, but you have to invest money to make money," she explains.

Mom plumps up the bed with the fancy tick quilt made by Great Aunt Ellen. She decorates the room with the baskets Grandma weaves from spruce roots. Finally she smacks her palms together. "There."

Grandma bumps her knee on the desk on her way into Eddie's room. She stands next to Mom, squinting. "It looks lovely. Your guests should be very comfortable, dear."

Eddie heads outside to call on Jake.

"I wouldn't want to sleep with my grandfather," Jake tells Eddie. He is riding the dented old bike they'd rescued from the dump. The boys are headed down the gravel road toward the park. "He snores louder than a jackhammer and he farts. And I sure wouldn't want just anyone staying in my room."

"Mom says we'll make more money in four months than in a whole year of fishing."

"It's too bad..." Jake starts to say something, but he doesn't finish.

"What's too bad?" prompts Eddie.

Jake stops riding. From where they stand on the small hill in the park, far to the east they can see the dark mass, which is the mainland. "I was just thinking it's too bad about your dad." He shrugs. "I mean, that you don't have him to go fishing with, like Fred."

Eddie knows Jake isn't trying to be mean, but he doesn't need to be told this either. For many reasons, life would be so much better if his dad was still around. Eddie's father had said he was tired of fishing when he'd boarded the ferry to the mainland a year earlier. He was off to find a more exciting job. Not a day went by that Eddie didn't think about him and wonder why he'd never come back.

"Oh, well," says Jake as he hops off the bike, "it's just the way it is. Maybe your mom's got a good idea. The Johnson's do the same thing. They take in tourists and they bought a computer last fall. Here, I'll set up the jump. You take the first run."

Eddie lies on a makeshift cot in Granddad's room, surrounded by all of their stuff. Eddie is waiting for Granddad to start snoring like a jackhammer. He's already opened the window in case he makes that other noise. So far, he's been quiet.

"Granddad?" Eddie whispers, realizing he also must still be awake.

"Yes, Eddie?"

"How come my dad never came back from the mainland?"

Granddad props himself up on an elbow. Eddie can see the outline of his thin body beneath the blanket in the pale light. "You know, I can't answer that for sure. But I think it has something to do with the mainland being like a crab trap."

"What do you mean?"

"Well, you know how a crab smells that bait and finds his way in. And once he's there, he finds that he's stuck. He could conceivably get out again the way he came in but he's confused and he can't figure it out."

"Oh," says Eddie. He remembers the last time he'd talked to his dad. As soon as he'd saved enough money, he'd told Eddie over the phone, he'd bring them all to the mainland. That was more than six months ago. "Do you think my dad might still figure it out?"

"It's possible."

Eddie hopes his dad is smarter than a crab. His mind drifts to something else. "Granddad?"

"Yes?"

"If I ever do see the big snapper—how will I know it's him?"

"Oh, now that I can answer. You'll know because you've never seen a snapper so big. But in case there's any doubt—you'll know by the notch in his dorsal fin. He got it from a run-in with my prop."

Eddie sits up suddenly, cross-legged on his cot. "When did that happen?"

"Let me see, now. That must have been close to forty years ago. I remember because it was shortly after your grandmother and I were married, but before your dad was born. I'd just finished building this cabin. I'd cut and planed every one of these cedar planks myself.

"We'd just moved in. I'd left your grandmother to putter around, arranging the furniture while I did a little fishing. A heavy mist had settled in some days before and made it difficult to see. I cut the engine about a mile out and began drifting. I thought I'd do a little trolling. The fog was thick but the water was calm and sounds carried a long way. In the distance, I heard a sea otter call for its mate. And closer at hand, I heard a humpback breathe.

"I'd already pulled in two good-sized flounders when I felt another fish tug on my line. I had a strong hunch it was that snapper. I could just tell by the way he grabbed hold of the lure then proceeded to steal my line. When he'd taken it all, he began dragging me along with him."

"Like the time he pulled you to Alcatraz?"

"Much like that. But this time, it was slower. And then, just like that, he stopped. I squinted into the fog and realized we were still in the bay. I wondered what had made him quit."

"Had you seen him yet?"

"Nope. It was still just a hunch that it was the snapper. But then—woosh!—there I was sitting fifty feet in the air in my skiff! That darn snapper had placed me right over the humpback's blowhole. And there he was, in the waves below, laughing through the mist."

"You were sitting on top of the whale's spout?"

"Well, yes, for a matter of a few seconds. But then that whale took a notion to dive. And it was sooner than the snapper must have thought, because he was now in the path of my falling boat. I'll tell you, that snapper's grin disappeared real quick. His eyes widened when he saw the boat coming at him and he did a couple of backstrokes before he turned to dive. Still, he wasn't quick enough. My boat hit the water. At the same time, the prop took a chunk of his dorsal fin. A small orange piece flew off. It was snatched from the air, gobbled up by a passing gull."

"What about you—were you hurt?"

"Me? Oh, no. I had friends who owed me a favor. The ones I leave the octopus on the rocks for when we're cleaning out the skiff at night. Half a dozen bald eagles spotted me pedaling in the air at the moment the whale dove. They swooped in to pluck me up like I was a sheet ready to be hung on the line. They carried me across the sound, and before I knew it, they'd deposited me on shore and taken off again into the sky. I turned just in time to see my basket and tackle drop back into my skiff."

"Wow," says Eddie.

"Your grandmother came out of the cabin at that moment. She plunked her hands on her hips and looked at me in a disapproving way. 'What are you doing standing here,' she asked, 'when

I can see your boat out there in the water?' She picked an eagle feather from my hair.

"Well, I tried to tell her, but she wouldn't have any of it. 'Stuff and nonsense! You expect me to believe your stories of giant snappers and friendly eagles?' She then accused me of being careless and letting my boat get away on its own."

Eddie is laughing loudly at Granddad's imitation of Grandma. Granddad chuckles along with him so that neither of them hears the sound of the bedroom door opening.

"What on earth is going on in here?!"

Startled, they both turn.

Mom stands in the doorway. She looks enormous in her puffy bathrobe and a mass of giant curlers parked on her head. Her forehead creases in a frown. "Will you two settle down? I hope you don't plan on carrying on like this when we have houseguests. Nobody will get a wink of sleep!"

Chapter 3

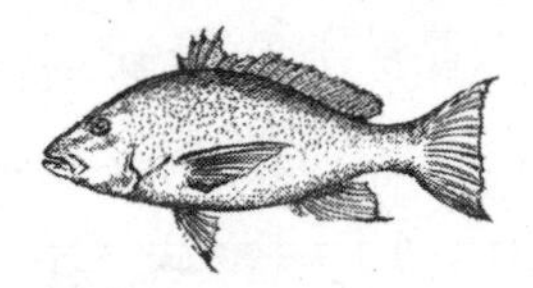

The Northorpes are staying in Eddie's room. There is Mr. Northorpe, who is thin and studious and is never without his binoculars. And there is Mrs. Northorpe, who is as restless as a bubble that can't settle on a place to land. She wants to know everything about the Queen Charlotte Islands and all the best places to visit. Whenever Granddad suggests a place, she runs for her map, which she spreads across the floor. The Northorpes also have a daughter named Becky. She is twelve years old, and to Eddie, appears totally bored with it all.

"You have a girl staying in your room?" Jake scoffs. It is the final day of school, and their backpacks are loaded with crumpled exercise books and brittle erasers cleaned out of their lockers. "How are you ever going to get it smelling normal again?"

Eddie shifts the weight on his back. He has already thought about this. "I thought I might do some wood burning. I'm thinking of making a name for the new skiff Granddad's building."

"What would you call it?"

Eddie doesn't take long to consider. "The Big Snapper."

"Yeah, I suppose that might work." Jake kicks a stone down the path. "I guess it depends on how long she stays."

Eddie has discovered that the worst part of having guests is not the space they occupy. It's the things you can't do in your own home. Like being impolite. Not that Eddie makes a habit of being impolite, but once in a while he picks the mushrooms from his chowder. Or he burps contentedly after downing a glass of Coke. Just to know that he can and that he won't get killed, like he would if he was eating in a restaurant. Since Mom started the bed and breakfast it's like eating every meal in a restaurant.

Becky Northorpe doesn't like fish. She doesn't like the taste or smell of it. And she hates the beach. She can't stand the crunch of barnacles beneath her sandals, and the hermit crabs scuttling between rocks give her the creeps. After beachcombing with her parents she uses up all the hot water in the cabin for a shower; then complains she still smells like sardines.

"I have an idea," Mom tells everyone at breakfast the next morning. "Mr. and Mrs. Northorpe are hiking to the Pesuta shipwreck today. Since Becky doesn't like the beach, Eddie, why don't you and Jake take her up to Spirit Lake?"

Eddie looks up with a start.

Mom is standing there, beaming, like she's just come up with the theory of relativity. Becky continues to pick Grandma's fry bread to shreds. Wearing broad hopeful grins, Mr. and Mrs. Northorpe have their eyes on Eddie.

"But I planned on going fishing with Granddad," ventures Eddie. "He needs my help."

"Oh, I think your grandfather can do without you for one day." Mom rises from the table and begins collecting plates. "What do you say, Granddad?"

Granddad agrees that he can manage, before glancing at Eddie. He raises his eyebrows in an apologetic way.

Mr. and Mrs. Northorpe drop Eddie, Becky

and Jake off at the bottom of the hill on their way to Naikoon Park.

Becky picks a stone from the toe of her sandal, tosses her blond ponytail over her shoulder and looks around. “So, where is this lake?”

“We have to hike to the top of that hill.” Eddie points to a break in the trees on the side of the road.

Becky rolls her eyes.

“How did you get sucked into this?” Jake whispers to Eddie as they start toward the path.

“I wasn’t given any choice.”

It is a beautiful, sunny day—there are not that many on the islands. The dark forest is full of bright shadows and dappled sunlight, and in places where the underbrush is thin, shafts of light reach through the tall cedars and illuminate the forest floor.

Becky doesn’t like the forest. Even on this particularly cheerful day when the recent rain has stirred up life, she thinks it’s dark and spooky and smells musty. Eddie has grown up with the odor of damp cedar and hemlock in his nose and it makes him feel at home.

Jake spots a tiny sitka deer standing in a bed

of ferns. He points it out to Becky, but she is busy complaining about the steepness of the hill and by the time she has turned, it is gone.

She shrugs and returns to the path. "So, what do you guys do for excitement around here?"

Eddie thinks about this. "Mostly fishing and crabbing. My granddad and I are building a fifteen foot—"

"Not those kinds of things," interrupts Becky. "I mean like stuff that you do for fun. Don't you have any shopping malls or movie theaters? It just seems so dead around here."

"Yeah, we wrestle grizzly bears," snorts Jake. "And when we're not doing that, we pull on wet suits and swim after hammerhead sharks."

Becky stops, opens her mouth a little, looks between Jake and Eddie and closes it again.

Eddie really wishes he was fishing with Granddad as they walk the final stretch to Spirit Lake. When they arrive, Becky is again not at all impressed.

"It's full of old logs and just spooky," she says, "and all that moss hanging from the trees looks like something gross and ugly sneezed."

Eddie tries to keep in mind that she's a girl, but even considering that disadvantage, he doesn't understand her distaste. He and Jake have spent hours, probably weeks if they added it up, building rafts and just hanging around Spirit Lake.

Becky finds a log just off the path overlooking the lake. She inspects it for bugs and sits down. Eddie swings the backpack off his shoulder and pulls out the sandwiches Grandma has made: smoked salmon for him and Jake, and, because she doesn't like fish, peanut butter for Becky. Jake wanders along the shore while Becky chews gingerly.

She drops the sandwich to her lap. "Man, what I wouldn't give for a Big Mac right now."

Eddie knows what a Big Mac is—he's seen it on TV. But he has never eaten one because there are no fast food restaurants where he lives.

Eddie's attention wanders from Becky to an eagle that is watching them from its nest in the tallest cedar across the lake. Like Eddie, it's probably trying to make sense of this chatty animal that has invaded its world. Eddie would really prefer to be down at the edge of the lake with Jake, launching the raft they'd made earlier in the year. But Becky is a guest, and he knows he'll never hear the end of it if he isn't polite.

When Eddie was younger, and Granddad was able to walk properly, the two of them would make the hike up to the lake almost every week.

"Have I ever told you how this lake was formed?" Eddie remembers Granddad asking him many years earlier. They had hiked about halfway up the path to the lake. Feeling particularly lazy that day, Eddie had been complaining about the climb and how far they still had to go.

Eddie didn't know how the lake was formed, but he guessed it might have been left behind by an ice mass, like he'd learned about in school. Many of North America's lakes had been created this way.

"Well, that's true. But not this one," Granddad had said. "It came to be during my great-great-grandfather's time. A tidal wave swept over the island. When the water receded, it took many things with it, but it also left some behind. Great-great Grandfather lost his home and his canoe, although fortunately, everyone in his family was safe.

"The morning after the flood, he set out in search of wood to build a new home. He was walking up this very same hill with his own grandson—my grandfather—who was about your age at the time. They felt the earth move. At first they thought they were in for another tidal wave, or perhaps an earthquake. But then it moved again, although this time it was accompanied by a rumbling sound. The rumbling turned to moaning and something like a groan. It sounded like someone, or something, was in pain. After following the sound, they broke through the woods into a clearing. Before them—right where Spirit Lake is now, lay a blue whale."

"Were they seeing things?" Eddie asked.

"Oh, no. It was a blue whale, all right. He'd been dropped by the tidal wave. Well, you can imagine the size of the depression one hundred tons of whale falling from the sky would leave. It was filled with water, but only just enough to have kept the whale alive. Great-great grandfather knew they'd have to do something quickly if the whale was to survive.

"So, the first thing he did was organize the children of the village to pass buckets of water up the hill to keep the whale damp. He then had the women sew hides together, working by the fire through the night, while the men cut a path from the top of the hill to the sea.

"All night, the whale continued to thrash around and the depression became quite a crater. By the next morning, everything was in place. It was a good thing too, because the whale was growing very weak. The men carried the hides the women had sewn to the top of the hill like a giant bolt of carpet. They rolled it down the path to the sea. Some of the people threw buckets of water over the hides while others dug next to the crater until the water began to flow. All at once, the whale came along with it. He slipped down that giant waterslide right back into the ocean while everyone cheered."

"Was this the path he slid along?" Eddie asked.

Granddad had said it was the very one. "Of course," he'd added, "it's grown over since then. You'd never be able to get a blue whale down it now. And the rain has filled the crater which you now know as Spirit Lake."

Becky is looking at Eddie. He realizes she has said something, and she's waiting for an answer.

"Sorry, what?"

Becky groans. "I asked you what's down that path?" Without waiting for an answer, she bounces from the log and starts to follow it. Eddie cannot resist any longer, and he joins Jake on the raft just as he is about to shove off. Spirit Lake is not a large lake and from any point they can see Becky moving through the trees where she follows the path encircling it.

Eddie and Jake push past the sunken cedars with long poles, headed toward the deeper water in the middle of the lake. They are leaning over the raft, their poles deep in the water, when a scream from Becky just about sends them overboard. They quickly scan the shore, but cannot see her.

"A mountain cat," Jake breathes.

Using their hands as paddles, and plunging their poles in the water, they furiously splash their way back to shore. They jump off where the water is knee deep, soaking their shoes and pants. Armed with their poles, Jake, followed closely by Eddie, climbs frantically back up to the path through the gooseberries, ignoring the scratches on his arms and face, intent on fending off a snarling cougar. After racing down the path, the boys run into Becky. She is just straightening up, brushing dirt from her knees and whimpering over a tear in her shorts.

"That root!" she sobs, pointing accusingly at a twisted old root protruding from the path. "It tripped me."

Jake and Eddie, dripping and breathless, glance at the innocent-looking root. In confusion, they look at each other.

"Well, someone should take better care of this path. It's hazardous. It's lucky I wasn't hurt." Becky turns and starts toward the main path leading down the hill.

"It could still happen," Jake growls, glaring after her.

Dragging their poles behind them, the boys return to the raft. After pulling it higher into the woods so it is safe between the trees, they follow Becky.

It is much easier climbing down the hill, but more difficult to listen to Becky, who seems to have more and more to say. Eddie suspects that her feelings about him and his family, and their home, have been accumulating and that her parents have been keeping her tongue in check. But after her run-in with the root, she's like a top wound tight and left to spin until it stops.

Jake doesn't feel the need to be as polite as Eddie. He asks if she is always such a motormouth.

She ignores him.

Jake walks ahead of them down the path. Becky asks Eddie where his father is.

"He went to the mainland, a year ago."

"And?"

"And," Eddie shrugs, "he hasn't come back."

He feels her eyes on him. "Well," she says, "I can't imagine living way out in the boondocks either if I had the choice. There's nothing to do and no place to go. And you're missing so many of the necessities. Like a computer. Where do you look stuff up? And how do you talk to your friends?"

Eddie is home in time to help Granddad with the boat. He secures it to its mooring and then lifts the gear and baskets to the wharf. Granddad has caught only two small rock cod.

"Takes me forever to bait that hook," he says apologetically to Eddie.

Eddie flips the lid on the basket. "Don't worry about it. I'll be with you tomorrow." He keeps pace with Granddad as he shuffles across the deck. Granddad stops briefly when he hears the sound of Eddie's sneakers, all squishy and wet.

"You fall off the path into the lake?"

Eddie frowns, "I don't want to talk about it."

Granddad lays an arm on his shoulder. They step from the wharf and start along the dirt path leading to the cabin.

"I've been thinking, Granddad." Eddie shifts the fishing rod in his hand. "Do you think I need a computer to talk to Jake?"

Chapter 4

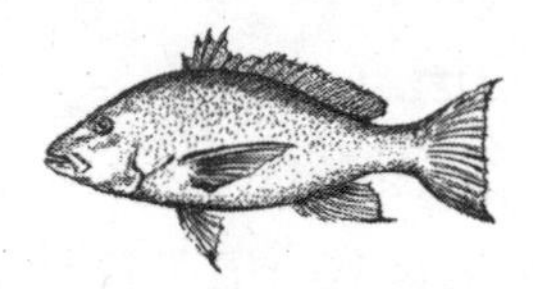

Eddie wakes up to the sound of rain beating hard against the roof. He glances at Granddad's empty bed then at the clock on the bookshelf across the room. He is surprised at how late it is. He hopes Granddad hasn't gone fishing without him. The Northorpes are going to the museum today so he is free of Becky, but he'd forgotten to tell Granddad.

Eddie dresses quickly. He finds Granddad sipping tea next to the fire in the sitting room. He doesn't look at all like he's prepared to go fishing. His legs are wrapped in a blanket and he wears his winter cardigan even though it is the end of June. "Good morning," he says on seeing Eddie.

"You didn't wake me up. Somebody will get our fishing spot."

"I thought maybe we could use a day off. Particularly you. You are on holidays, aren't you? Besides, it's raining."

Eddie cannot remember a time when Granddad has been stopped by a little rain. If rain played a part in their decision to go fishing, they would spend ninety percent of the year in the cabin. "Are you sure?"

"Yes, he's sure," Mom answers from the kitchen. She is rolling dough with determined strokes. "Your granddad's not feeling well today. He overdid it yesterday. He's getting too old to be gadding about in boats and lugging in fish all by himself. He's spending the day right there, and I'm going to see to it that he doesn't move."

Eddie looks to Granddad for confirmation. He smiles apologetically, telling Eddie that he has already resigned himself to do as Mom says.

"What about working on the boat?" Eddie asks.

Again, Mom answers for Granddad. "Nope, he won't be doing that either." She wipes her hands on her apron. "Eddie, come and eat your cereal. Then why don't you go see what Jake's up to today?"

Eddie is terribly disappointed. Two days in

a row he's missed fishing. All spring he'd been looking forward to the summer and fishing every day with Granddad. He's spent hours imagining what they might catch.

After he eats, Eddie splashes down the path that leads beneath the trees between the cabins. The rain is not falling as heavily as it had sounded to Eddie from inside the house, but the world around him is certainly drenched. He stiffens when water from the dripping branches makes its way down his collar and the back of his neck.

Jake lives farther along the shore, closer to the village than the Jamesons. He lives with his older sister, Peggy, and her husband, Fred. Jake's father was drowned in a terrible storm when Jake was only two. His mother lives in the village in a tiny house next to the General Market. She is very old for a mother, much older than Eddie's own mother. When she began to have trouble caring for Jake, Peggy and Fred invited him to live with them. Eddie likes Fred very much. He is good to the two boys, and he's always right there when Granddad needs help moving something heavier than Eddie can lift. Today, Fred and Jake are delivering a load of firewood to Jake's mother.

Jake and Eddie carry the split cedar to Fred who stands in the back of the truck and piles it up. He covers it with a tarp, so that pieces don't fly into the windshields of vehicles behind them, and they crowd into the cab. The truck bounces in the deep ruts now overflowing with water. Fred laughs and tells them that people on the main land pay big money for rides like this.

When they arrive at Mrs. Greenshaw's house, they unload the wood into the woodshed. Eddie gets a sliver in the palm of his hand. Mrs. Greenshaw has him sit at the kitchen table.

"Now hold still, Eddie. Just watch those two out the window and make sure they don't get into trouble."

Through the kitchen window, Eddie watches Jake and Fred stacking wood. He sees Mrs. Greenshaw's dog, Flounder, steal a stick of fire-wood from the shed. Fred sees it too and runs after him, but he slips and falls on his butt on the wet grass. Flounder drops the stick and wags his tail, waiting for someone to chase him. He seems to think that by falling down Fred is trying to get out of the game. Eddie laughs. Mrs. Greenshaw has removed the sliver with tweezers. She is rubbing Eddie's palm with some kind of berries pounded into a paste and mixed with oil.

"There, now. That should heal in no time. Now tell me, what's wrong that you aren't fishing with your granddad today?"

Mrs. Greenshaw knows Granddad fishes every day and that when school is out, Eddie goes with him. She knows the routines of everyone in the village and when they're not followed she likes to know why.

"He's not feeling very well."

"Oh? What's wrong with him?"

"He's worn out. Mom says he overdid it fishing by himself yesterday."

Mrs. Greenshaw holds a finger before her lips and frowns. "How is his walking?"

"Still slow."

She turns and ponders her shelf of bottles and jars. Mrs. Greenshaw makes ointments and medicine from plants, berries and roots in the same way that her Haida ancestors did. Jake and Eddie often go with her into the woods to help search for what she needs. They dig up spruce roots and pick licorice fern, which is good for colds and sore throats. They gather wild crab apples, devil's club and fireweed. Mrs. Greenshaw scrapes or boils the bark and pounds the berries. She's always got pots and kettles simmering on the stove. She now reaches for a jar of something that looks like ash.

"Tell your granddad to add a good heaping spoonful of this to his tea three times a day."

Eddie takes the jar and thanks her.

"How is his shaking?"

"It seems to be getting worse. He only caught two rock cod yesterday because he has trouble getting the octopus on the hook."

"Hmm. Well, how are his stories? Is he still telling stories?"

"Oh, yes."

"Good." Mrs. Greenshaw nods. "As long as he's telling stories there's nothing to worry about. When those stop, that's when we'll get concerned. Go get Fred and Jake now; I've made fish soup for lunch."

It is still raining after dinner, and the Northorpes, who returned in the late afternoon from the museum, are restless. Well, it's mostly Becky that can't sit still. The family is sitting with Eddie and Granddad by the fire in the sitting room. Granddad is sipping tea with a teaspoon of the ash mixed in it. Mom and Grandma are in the kitchen making jam. The air in the cabin is not only damp, it is now sweet and heavy from the boiling fruit.

Mrs. Northorpe has just commented on how nice it is to listen to the rain and be able to read a book without any distractions. Mr. Northorpe is busy studying an old map of the island Granddad had found. Becky is squirming in a chair, making a cat's cradle with the cord to her headphones.

"I can't even go for a walk," she complains.

Eddie doesn't understand what's preventing her. So she gets a little wet. Mr. Northorpe obviously has the same thought. Without glancing up from the map, he says, "Why not?"

Becky drops the headphones. "In case you haven't noticed, Dad, it's raining. Besides, it's dark and I might run into a bear."

"I don't think that's very likely. Why don't you ask Mr. Jameson what the chances are of that?"

Eddie turns to Granddad at the same time as Becky does. It has bothered him to see his grandfather sitting in the same place all day, nodding off, while the fishing boats came and went. It has worried him how little interest Granddad showed as each fisherman unloaded his catch on the wharf. He remembers what Jake's mom had said about Granddad and there being no need to worry as long as he is telling stories. He wonders how Granddad will answer Becky.

"Well, I did see a large bear late last fall. He passed behind this row of cabins more than once."

"Oh, what type of bear?" Mr. Northorpe asks.

"A black bear. A big one. Close to eight hundred pounds, I'd guess. I would imagine he'd stand about twelve feet if he was on his hind legs."

"Really?" says Becky. "But that's taller than this ceiling. It's taller than the two of you together."

Mr. Northorpe laughs. "I think Mr. Jameson may be exaggerating. I don't think black bears get that big. Now, maybe a grizzly. Are you sure it wasn't a grizzly?"

Granddad sips his tea slowly as he considers this. "Well, maybe. I suppose I could have made a mistake."

Eddie can't believe what he is hearing. Granddad could tell a grizzly from a black bear a hundred feet away in the dark. If there *were* any wild grizzlies on Graham Island, which there are not.

“What happened to him?” Becky asks.

Again, Granddad is slow to answer. “I don’t know. He just stopped coming around.”

“Oh,” says Becky. “Well, there you go. Now I really can’t go for a walk. If anyone wants me I’m going to be in my room listening to music.” Becky positions the earphone plugs in her ears, bounces to Eddie’s room and slams the door.

Chapter 5

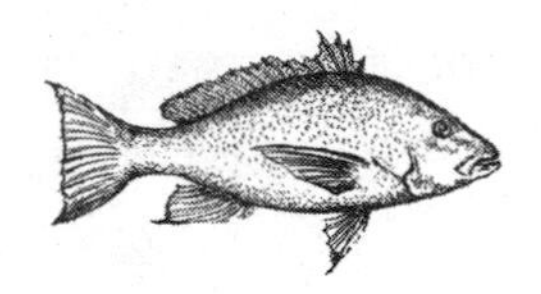

The Northorpes leave the island three days later. They have never seen so much rain in all their lives, and they have no idea how people can live in a place so damp. Eddie is relieved.

He imagines Becky at home talking to her friends over her computer, taking bites of a Big Mac as she types. She's just had the most hideous vacation. They traveled all that way and there was absolutely nothing to do. No proper restaurants, no theaters or shopping malls, and the walking paths were absolute death traps. It was so wet you could rarely leave the cabin, and everything smelt like fish!

Granddad says Mrs. Greenshaw's medicine has helped him and he is feeling more chipper.

He sits at the kitchen table wearing his fishing vest on the morning after the Northorpes leave.

When Eddie sees this, he immediately runs back to the room they share for his own fishing jacket. He had just assumed they wouldn't be going fishing again today. He then bolts down his breakfast while Grandma tells him to stop wolfing down his food and that even Flounder has more manners.

When they are ready, Grandma hands them the thermos and the basket of sandwiches she has made. "Now, Granddad," she calls after them as they head out the door, "you be sure and mind Eddie."

Eddie isn't sure why she says this, but she does, every time they leave the house.

Eddie and Granddad carry their gear down to the wharf. It has stopped raining, although a heavy layer of fog hangs low in the sky. They nod to the other fishermen. Granddad listens to remarks about where the fish are biting and what type of bait they're going for. They then climb aboard the skiff. Once the gear and baskets are stowed, Granddad starts the engine, and thirty minutes later they are drifting in the foggy bay, waiting for a tug on the line.

Eddie's heart is much lighter now that Granddad is feeling better. He had been worried that something was seriously wrong. When Granddad had told the Northorpes about the bear he'd seen, he hadn't done much explaining. He'd just said that the bear had stopped coming around. This was not like Granddad, and again, Eddie remembers what Mrs. Greenshaw said about not getting worried until the stories stopped.

"You've never told me about the bear you saw behind the cabin," Eddie says. "The one you told the Northorpes about."

Granddad laughs. "Well, perhaps I haven't. Probably because you were just a little trout in diapers at the time."

"Was it a black bear?"

"Of course it was. It was Trotter. The old black with the gray snout we see down at the mouth of the river. He and I have been fishing side by side for more than thirty years."

"Oh," says Eddie. But he wonders why Granddad hadn't insisted it was a black bear when Mr. Northorpe had doubted Trotter's size.

Granddad reels in a little line. There is no resistance. "Do you want to hear the story?"

"Yes," Eddie answers.

"It was, as I said, when you were a little guy. About ten years ago. I was down on the wharf loading my tackle when I spotted Trotter loping down the road past the cabins. I didn't think much of it at the time. Not until I was done for the day and coming back in when there he was again, only this time, he was going the other way. The next day the same thing happened. And the day after that. I began to keep a careful watch. Nearly a month went by and Trotter was making the trip back and forth at least three times a day. You know those ruts in the road?"

Eddie nods.

"They were caused by him—all his pacing. Well, it got to be near the end of December and I wondered why he hadn't turned in for the winter like all the other bears. So the next day, I followed him. I kept some distance back, ducking behind bushes when he turned. But even as far back as I was, I could see that his eyes were bloodshot and the skin beneath puffed and sagging. Under normal circumstances he would have sensed that I was there, but he was preoccupied, and I realized he was too tired and grumpy to care. He lashed out at branches that annoyed him and he grumbled at anything that crossed his path.

"I followed him to the foot of a rock overhang. The cliff was undercut. Beneath it was a cave with a mass of twisted roots hiding the entrance. It was Trotter's den. While I watched from behind a tree, he stood before it and let out the most distressing bellow you can imagine an animal made of flesh and blood could create. He then turned and headed back in the direction from which we'd come."

"Why didn't he go inside?" Eddie asks.

"Exactly what I wondered. So, once he had left, I got closer and peeked inside the den. There was nothing in it other than his bed of trampled branches and leaves. But while I was in there, the earth began to rumble and the walls began to shake. Well, you can imagine, I got out fast. The sound of machinery grinding and timber cracking became louder. It was a bulldozer, followed by the scream of a chainsaw. They were logging the forest above Trotter's den. He couldn't sleep because of all the noise."

"Poor Trotter."

"Yes, poor Trotter. But it also occurred to me

that if Trotter didn't get his sleep, he might not be so agreeable about sharing his fishing ground in the spring. I couldn't exactly move his den. The only thing to do was to get the loggers to move away. I climbed the hill to the part of the forest where they were logging and approached a fellow who looked like he might be in charge. Well, he laughed when I suggested they move somewhere else because they were disturbing the sleep of a bear. So did all the men working with him when he told them what I'd said.

"I didn't want to resort to anything nasty, but I knew I'd have to force them out. I watched how they went about their work. The fellow I'd talked to—he was, indeed, the foreman—would go ahead of the others and tie markers around the trees he wanted cut. I knew exactly what I had to do. I went home and had your grandmother sew me a costume of hides. 'I want it fifteen feet high,' I said. 'What on earth for?' she asked me. 'That's nearly three times as big as you.' I told her to never mind, she'd find out.

"While she was doing that, I carved a mask—a hideous face with long teeth and bulging eyes."

"What were you going to do with it?"

"Just wait. You'll find out. When that part of

the costume was ready, I covered my snowshoes in rubber from an old tire so they looked like very large boots. Then I gathered everything together. Well before dawn, I started toward the area where they were logging. At the edge of the woods where I found the last cut tree, I pulled on the snowshoes and walked through the trees in the moonlight, leaving enormous footprints in the snow as I went. I found a cedar tree about fifteen feet high and dressed it in the costume your grandmother had sewn. I fit the mask I had made in place. I had brought along some long poles. With these, I could manipulate the branches to give the impression that the arms and legs were moving. I then waited for day to break and the logging crew to arrive.

"The sun was barely up when they pulled up in their trucks. The men working the equipment got it ready, while the fellow who selected the trees started out. I could see him from where I waited behind the cedar. He came across my first footprint and stopped. He looked ahead and saw another. Slowly, he followed them, glancing around as he walked. He was maybe a hundred yards away when he spotted the cedar dressed in the costume your grandmother had made. I jabbed hard at the branches with my poles so that the arms and legs began to dance. The foreman's eyes opened wide. 'Sasquatch!' he hollered, loud enough to be heard on the mainland. 'It's a sasquatch! Everybody, clear out!' He then turned and ran faster than a swift fox."

Eddie laughs loudly.

"Well, there was no question if the others believed him or not. He was so terrified they knew he must have seen something. After all, he was the boss and they had confidence in him. So they packed up their equipment and left the site. And Trotter didn't come around anymore. When I checked on him, he was fast asleep."

When Granddad is finished, Eddie thinks about what he has said. "Granddad, why didn't you tell Mr. Northorpe you knew it wasn't a grizzly and that there aren't any grizzly bears on the island?"

Granddad considers his answer. "Because, Eddie, Mr. Northorpe likes to read and he is proud of all he knows. And he was a guest in our house."

Eddie is reassured that Granddad is still telling stories. But he also wonders if the Northorpes

would have thought their island was less boring if they'd heard about Trotter, the sasquatch and how the ruts came about.

Chapter 6

By noon, Granddad and Eddie have landed five silver salmon between ten and fifteen pounds each. After they eat their sandwiches, Eddie takes the rod while Granddad settles in for a snooze.

"Now remember, if you get a strike don't pull too hard or too fast," he tells Eddie. He plumps up a lifejacket and lies back on it, folds his hands over his chest and closes his eyes.

The fog has burned off, and Eddie waves at a passing tour boat. He looks toward the shoreline where he watches Jake and Fred tie up at the wharf. He is too far out in the bay to distinguish everyone, but he recognizes Fred, who towers above all the other fishermen, and Jake, who is wearing his Masset fishing derby hat. Flounder bounds from the boat to the wharf.

Eddie is adjusting his own hat when he gets a hit. A bit of a tug and a moment of slack, and then the fish strikes again. In a matter of seconds the line is taut. Eddie allows a little more line to peel off. He doesn't pull too hard, or too fast—in fact, the fish quickly uses up the extra line he gives it, and it's all he can do to hold on to it. "Granddad, you'd better wake up."

Granddad opens one eye. Eddie is hanging on to that rod with all his might. His upper body pivots in the direction the fish takes. Granddad sits up and quickly slides next to him. "Let him take it, Eddie. Give him lots of line and lots of space. We've got the whole ocean to wear him out."

Eddie realizes this is true. He lets the reel free-spool for a time.

The fish changes directions again, pulling Eddie's arm at an unnatural angle as it crosses to the other side beneath the boat. Granddad takes the rod. This allows Eddie a chance to straighten up and shake the tingling out of his arm. "Let me have it back."

"Are you sure?"

"Yes."

Granddad passes the rod back to Eddie. The short break has renewed the strength in his arms as well as his determination. He listens to Granddad's directions, but he is also taking directions from the fish. After a time, when he has given the fish as much line as he can afford, he tries to raise it just a little, but the line will still not yield.

Fifteen minutes pass. Eddie's arms are numb and his shoulders are feeling the strain. He wants to pass the rod to Granddad again, but this is his fish and he is determined to land it himself. It is a big fish, Eddie can feel it. The biggest he's ever hooked.

"Are you okay?" Granddad asks.

Eddie nods. The effort to answer would take energy away from what he needs to land the fish.

Thirty more minutes elapse and looking up, Eddie realizes they have moved some distance out into the bay. His back is cramped and he cannot feel his arms. But at least he's now able to gain a few feet of line back from the fish. And by the angle of the line it appears the fish is rising—slowly, but it's happening.

"Don't give up, now," Granddad tells him. "Keep the tension on him. Let him know who's boss."

"I'm trying to, but he's really strong."

"And so are you. At least you can make him think that you are."

"He's big, Granddad."

"Yes, he is. But he doesn't need to know that you're not. He doesn't need to know you're just a boy. Make him think you are a very big man."

Eddie stands tall and tries to make him think just that. He also tries not to let the fish know that he is scared and very sore.

He is able to gain line steadily now, a small bit at a time. He guesses the fish still has about twenty yards. Granddad stands at his side ready with the gaff and club, although they have still not seen the fish. It has been an hour since Eddie felt the first tug.

Suddenly, the line lurches, and Eddie is catapulted forward. Granddad drops the gaff and grabs him tightly around the waist. Eddie is surprised at his strength. Then, just as suddenly, there is no resistance—Granddad and Eddie find they are pulling hard against nothing at all. Eddie is pitched back like he's been shot out of a slingshot. He stumbles against Granddad, who softens his fall against the floor of the skiff.

Eddie sits there a moment as stunned as a newly caught fish. "I lost him," he says.

"Yes," says Granddad, pulling him to his feet. "You did. But you gave him a good fight. Something he can tell his friends about."

Despite his disappointment, Eddie grins. He stands up and brushes himself off. Granddad reels in the line then he hands the rod to Eddie to attach a new leader and a piece of octopus. He hauls in the anchor and starts the engine to drive them back to shallower water. Eddie doesn't notice that it seems to take an unusual amount of effort for him to pull the starter cord. Twice, three times it takes Granddad to get the engine chugging.

Eddie feels the wind in his hair and the spray on his face as they cross the bay. He can't wait to tell Jake and Fred about the fish he almost caught. He'll tell them how it pulled them far out of the bay. He'll describe how it nearly yanked him overboard, but Granddad was able to save him at the last minute.

Granddad cuts the engine about the place they started out. He drops the line again.

Eddie begins to wonder what would have

happened if Granddad hadn't been able to grab him. What if the fish had pulled him right out of the boat? He imagines himself flying out of the skiff, skiing behind the fish across the water, just like he was being pulled by a powerboat. The fish was that strong. Perhaps they would get going so fast he would become airborne. This would certainly confuse the gulls and the eagles as well as the passengers on any passing boats: a boy flying through the air like a kite, with nothing holding him up, or towing him, because the line would be invisible from any distance. It would be a wonderful story, and he can just imagine the look on Jake's face.

"I never saw it," Eddie suddenly says.

"No," says Granddad. "He didn't give us the chance. But I bet he was half the size of this boat. I've become a pretty good judge of the size of a fish just by the way it fights."

Eddie has a thought. "Do you think it was the big snapper?"

Granddad considers this. "No, it wasn't the big snapper. At least, not the one that I know. That isn't how he operates. He makes you use your head, not just your muscle."

"Oh." Eddie is a little disappointed.

"Of course," says Granddad, testing the line. "It could have been one of his kids. Just feeling his way. The way he pulled hard on the line and then let it snap back—now that's something the snapper might have done in his younger days."

"The snapper has kids?"

"Yeah, he has kids, three that I know of. Have I never told you about the time he chased me away when I stumbled on to them?"

Eddie shakes his head.

"Hmm. Let's see, it was fifteen years ago, give or take a few. In the bay, on the other side of the point here, I was doing a little trolling. The water's always a little choppier around there because of the wind. But in one spot, it seemed choppier than usual. When I came up to it, that one spot was boiling with fish. Snappers—I figured it must have been a whole school of them—they'd come up to the surface to mess around a bit. But as I watched, I realized it wasn't a whole school at all, there were really only a few. They were just particularly rambunctious: playing some kind of fish tag, madly chasing each other around, back and forth, leaping between the waves, creating a lot of foam.

"Well, I didn't waste any time, you can be sure

of that. I dropped my anchor and cast, right into the middle of their game. As my bait disappeared beneath the waves, they stopped and watched after it. The water settled, and I could now clearly see three small snappers: two with frilly dorsal fins and one with an attitude and slicked back pectorals and tail. One of the frilly-tailed fry, a little bolder than the other, swam after the octopus and disappeared from sight. I waited for a tug on the line. Well, you can imagine how surprised I was when, instead of a tug, my hull was broadsided by what felt like a hammerhead shark. It hit so hard my skiff jumped fifty feet, like a stone skipping across the water. This dent right here..." Granddad taps a dent the size of a watermelon in the side of the skiff with his foot. "That's where I was hit."

"What hit you?" Eddie asks.

"Why, the snapper. Don't know where he came from. Maybe he'd been out hunting for mollusks and thought the kids were safe. Well, I no sooner had a chance to get the anchor up and the engine started when he rammed into me again. And as you boys say when you're playing basketball—this time it got me some air. I flew right over the point in my skiff, clear across the beaches on both sides and the cottages and woods between. When I peeked over the gunwale, people were gazing into the sky, rubbing their eyes and blinking.

"I landed right next to Fred who was out fishing. He was sprawled in the stern with one leg draped over the boat, his fishing hat over his face, and I think he was probably asleep. Woke him up quick though. I landed with a great splash that set his boat rocking. He jumped up so that his hat flew off and he stubbed his toe getting his leg into his boat. 'Geez, Ben,' he said to me, 'you shouldn't sneak up on a guy like that.'

"Well, I guess I looked a little shook-up myself because then he asked, 'Are you all right?' I looked around to make sure that I was, that all my body parts and fishing gear had landed in the skiff along with me. When I was certain they had, I told him that I was. He then looked at me sort of quizzically, 'The snapper?' he asked. 'The snapper,' I said.

"Anyway, it taught me not to tangle with anything protecting its young. Look here, Eddie. I think we've got another bite. Nothing like what you hooked, but your mom's going to be happy with us tonight."

Eddie helps Granddad bring in another salmon. Granddad is right; it's not anywhere near the size of the fish that almost pulled Eddie from the boat.

On the way back to the wharf, he thinks of Granddad's story. He thinks of how his own dad is not around to protect him. Not that he needs it particularly, but today, it was a good thing Granddad was there.

Chapter 7

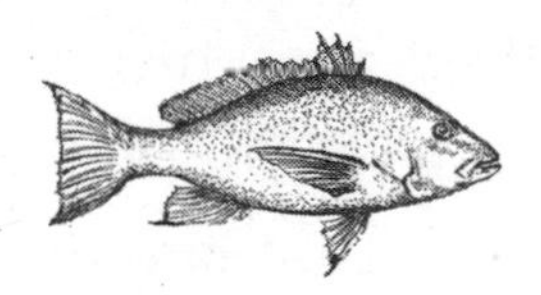

The following morning, Granddad cannot get out of bed. He is very tired and his legs refuse to do what he wants. Even when Mrs. Greenshaw is summoned with her basket of ointments and pills, nothing seems to help. Finally, Dr. Gibson visits just before lunch. He examines Granddad and then tells him he must go to the medical clinic and have some tests done after he's had a chance to rest.

Eddie remembers Granddad hanging onto him with the strength of an ironman so he wouldn't fly out of the boat. He wonders how he could do that one day and be so weak he can't stand on his feet the next. Eddie begins to worry that Granddad is weak because he used up all his strength rescuing him. For this reason he finds it difficult to accept the congratulations that keep coming his way.

"I hear you almost caught a whale yesterday." Dr. Gibson cuffs Eddie on the shoulder. "Taking after your granddad. Way to go, sport."

Mom almost squeezes the Shredded Wheat right out of him, and Fred gives him the thumbs-up on his way to the wharf. Grandma says he's a chip off the old block—by that she means Granddad.

A new family moves into Eddie's room after lunch. Mr. and Mrs. Backhouse and their eight-year-old twin boys. Eddie quickly discovers that the twins are even more annoying than Becky Northorpe. By mid-afternoon they are already complaining there's nothing to do. Mr. Backhouse suggests they take a walk down to the wharf. Eddie watches them through the window. The twins are throwing mussels at each other and chasing the sandpipers with sticks.

At five minutes to four, Fred and Eddie help Granddad into the truck. He is not strong enough to walk to his appointment at the medical clinic in the village. Fred does some errands while Eddie throws a ball for Flounder in Mrs. Greenshaw's yard where Jake is polishing their old wreck of a bike.

"I wish I'd been there when you caught that fish yesterday," Jake tells him. "It must have been so cool. Maybe if I'd been there we would have been strong enough to haul it in together."

"Maybe," Eddie says.

"What are you doing after supper? We should go to the dump and look for a new chain for our bike. This one falls off every twenty feet."

Flounder drops the ball at Eddie's feet. He throws it for the ninety-ninth time. "If you want."

"And some handlebar grips. These ones are shot. Look at this, the rubber is all dried out."

"Yeah," says Eddie. "I wonder what's taking Granddad so long."

Flounder is lying next to Jake and Eddie on the grass, his tongue hanging out like an old balloon, when Fred and Granddad pull up in the truck.

Eddie and Jake climb in. "So, what did he say?" Eddie wipes dog slobber off his hands onto his pants.

"Dr. Gibson says I'll be fine," Granddad answers, "with a bit of rest and some treatments."

"Oh," says Eddie. He wonders what kind of treatments, but Granddad says he'll be just fine and that's what's important, so he leaves it at that. He does seem to be feeling a little better. Even so, Mom and Grandma order him back to bed as soon as they arrive home.

All through dinner, the Backhouse twins complain about the food Grandma has cooked. They prod the smoked salmon with their forks and poke their spoons in the shredded kelp soup. They tell their parents everything's just too weird to eat. Eddie can't think of anything less weird than kelp; it's as common as rain where he lives. Mr. Backhouse tries to shush them, but he's not very good at it. And Mrs. Backhouse seems too worn-out to say anything at all.

But Grandma doesn't notice, or if she does, it doesn't appear to bother her. She's got other things on her mind. She's wearing new glasses, and everywhere she looks, she's discovering things she's never noticed. In some ways this is good—she hasn't tripped or bumped into anything since she picked them up from the drugstore. But she's also noticing things that Eddie thought were just fine the way they were.

"Eddie, is that a hole I see in your jeans?" she'd asked just before dinner. "Good heavens, yes, it is! You take those pants off right now so I can mend them before anyone sees you like that."

Eddie had taken the pants off, although it was far too late to be seen without the hole. It had been there through most of the school year.

Eddie helps clear the table after dinner before heading to Jake's and the dump. "Eddie," Grandma says as he's about to go out the door. She stands before the kitchen sink, washing dishes. "Don't you leave this house without tying your shoes. I can hear the laces slapping on the floor. You'll trip and break your neck."

Eddie looks down at his runners. The laces are knotted and they do trail along the cabin floor. He bends down to tie them. At the same time he wonders how a new pair of glasses can sharpen a person's hearing. It's not easy to get them unknotted and tied up properly because he hasn't used them in ages, and although he's tripped many times, he's certainly never broken his neck.

Seagulls circle above the dump, dozens of them, screaming at Jake and Eddie. The boys have to climb a chain-link fence built to keep Trotter and the other bears out. Once they're inside, they scout for old bikes in the new garbage. They know all the bikes and who owns them in the village, but now and again a tourist will toss one out. There are no new bikes, but Jake stumbles on a wooden wagon the size of a small tub.

"It's got a broken axle," he says after inspecting it, "but if we fix that, we can hitch it to the bike so neither of us has to walk."

Eddie thinks this is a great idea. They could take turns between riding the bike and riding in the wagon. They then struggle to get it over the fence before the sky turns very dark.

Eddie lies in bed thinking about how they're going to fix the broken axle. Granddad is not snoring so he also must still be awake. Eddie tells him about the wagon and asks his opinion on how to fix it.

"Where is it?" Granddad asks.

"It's in the boat shed."

With some difficulty, Granddad swings his legs over the bed and sits up. "I'll tell you what. If we can sneak past your mother and grandmother, I'll take a look."

"Right now?"

“They’re in their bedroom. I can’t get past them during the day, so now’s our only chance.”

Eddie tiptoes to the door and opens it. The hall to the kitchen and the back door is dark. He signals for Granddad to follow. Granddad slips on his leather slippers and pads after him. They reach the back door where, as quietly as he can, Eddie turns the knob. Once they are outside, the moon is uncharacteristically bright, illuminating the yard. Eddie ducks beneath branches and keeps to the shadows as he leads the way across the damp grass. Granddad follows. They are almost across the yard when Granddad is forced to stop and catch his breath. Briefly, he leans on the table where he fillets fish.

“Ready?” Eddie asks when he hears Granddad’s breathing lighten.

“Ready,” Granddad says.

They continue on together and enter the shed as quietly as they’d left the house. Eddie does not turn on the light until both of them are inside and the door is closed.

The shed smells strongly of cedar. The hull of the boat Granddad’s been working on over the past two years is supported by sawhorses in the center of the room. Curly wood shavings litter the floor and the walls are hung with tools.

"So, where is it?" Granddad asks.

Eddie points to the other side of the boat, to the big wooden wagon he and Jake had salvaged from the dump.

Granddad whistles—softly so Grandma can't possibly hear him. "What are you boys planning to haul in that thing?"

"We're going to hitch it to the bike and pull each other around."

Granddad steps closer. "Why, it's as big as a taxi cab. You could start a business and charge people to take them around town."

Eddie had never thought of that. He envisions Mrs. Greenshaw stepping into the wagon, tucking her long skirts around her, clutching her bag of medicines and herbs, and Eddie jumping on the bike, waiting for her instructions, and pulling her to the home of whoever is sick.

Granddad inspects the wagon and axle. "All it needs is a new rivet. I've got what we need right here."

Eddie helps Granddad flip the wagon and he brings him the tools he needs. When he's finished fastening the rivet, they flip the wagon upright again. After a shot of WD-40, it rolls smoothly, and Eddie is pleased. Granddad climbs aboard to test it. Eddie laughs at the sight of his old grandfather sitting in the wagon like he's a little kid. He pulls him once around the boat.

They sneak back to the house along the same route they'd taken to the shed. Granddad stops more often to rest. Eddie waits each time before moving forward again.

Eddie is the first one in the back door. The kitchen light flicks on abruptly, even though he is not even near the switch.

Grandma stands in the doorway in her nightgown; her arms are crossed and her silver hair is a fuzzy mess. She stares at them, her blue eyes wide behind her new glasses. "Just where have you two been?"

Eddie and Granddad are too surprised to say anything immediately.

"Granddad was helping me with a project," Eddie finally explains.

She glares at Granddad. "You know you're not to get out of bed." She then turns to Eddie. "And you're not to be encouraging him. Now both of you, back to bed."

Eddie and Granddad tiptoe past Grandma

and down the hall again, even though there is no longer any reason to sneak.

Twenty minutes later, Eddie is lying in bed thinking about the fixed axle. Granddad seems to know he's not asleep.

"Eddie?"

"Yes, Granddad?"

"I want to tell you a little more about the treatments Dr. Gibson says I'm going to need."

Eddie sits up. So does Granddad.

"They have to be done in a big city hospital. It means I'm going to have to go to the mainland for a while."

"How long?"

"Six weeks."

This unexpected news causes Eddie's stomach to twist and his throat to tighten.

"You said you were going to be just fine," he says.

"Dr. Gibson thinks I will. But it is very important that I have the treatments."

Eddie wants Granddad to be well, but six weeks is a very long time. He'll be back at school by the time Granddad's home again. His eyes begin to sting along with the pain in his stomach. If he comes home at all.

"Eddie, I know what you're thinking. I will come home. Don't you ever think that I won't."

Eddie wipes away the tear rolling down his cheek. He's glad it's dark and that Granddad can't see his face.

Chapter 8

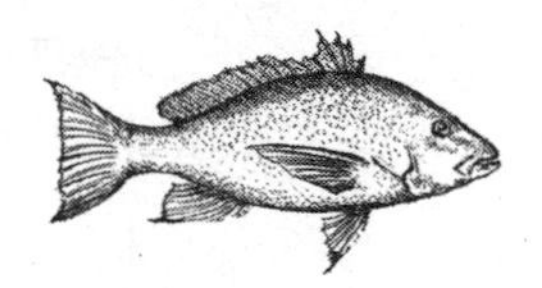

The Backhouse family leaves the island a few days later. Two more couples come and go before the end of the week. Finally it's Granddad's turn. The morning he is to leave, Eddie helps him pack his suitcase. They try to discuss what he'll need for the hospital, but they can't hear each other above Mom vacuuming. She's vacuumed every day—sometimes even twice a day—since she bought her new Hoover from the hardware store. Grandma is going with Granddad. She'll be staying with some cousin Eddie has never heard of.

"I wish I could come too," Eddie shouts as he passes Granddad a pair of socks from his dresser drawer.

Thankfully, the noise of the vacuum cleaner stops.

Granddad puts the socks in his suitcase. "I know. But you'd be more bored than a day of fishing without a bite. Dr. Gibson says the treatments will make me a little sick, and I'm not going to be able to leave the hospital. And Grandma will be too busy fussing and driving me crazy to take you around."

"Are you scared?" Eddie asks. He knows he would be if it was him. "I mean, you're going to a strange place to have treatments that you already know will make you sick."

"Scared? Are you kidding? I'll be warm and dry. Maybe the food won't be so great but at least I won't starve to death. And if that's all I have to put up with to get better, it's worth the price. This is going to be a breeze compared to some of the situations I've faced in my life."

Eddie tries to think of one of the scarier situations Granddad has been in. The trick he'd played on the loggers sounded a bit scary. What if he'd been caught? But Granddad hadn't told the story like it was. "Like what?" he asks.

"Hmm. Well, like the time I stumbled into the middle of a mutiny."

"You stumbled into a mutiny?"

"I haven't told you that story?"

Eddie shakes his head.

Granddad appears surprised. He stops packing for the moment and sits down on the bed. "This goes way back. I was probably not much older than you at the time."

Eddie tries to imagine Granddad ten years old. He can picture him shorter and wearing jeans and a T-shirt. But it's still Granddad's wrinkled face with wisps of thin gray hair sprouting from under a baseball cap.

"I had a good friend named Rick. One early November day, we took a walk out to Rose Spit. The fog was as thick as your Grandma's chowder; nevertheless, we hiked up to the top of Tow Hill. On a clear day, you can see east as far as the mainland and north all the way to Alaska. But on that day we could barely see our hands at the ends of our arms.

"We climbed down and walked along the shore. The rocks were slippery, slick with weeds and still wet from the tide rolling out. We stopped to see what had been left behind by the tide. Rick was behind me. I was squatting to inspect a pool when he called me. I turned to see what he wanted and lost my footing. I hadn't realized how close to the edge I was. Suddenly I was falling, down through the fog, unable to see what was below me. I hoped to hit water, but I also braced myself to hit rock.

"As it happened, I didn't hit either. After falling for what seemed an eternity, I hit something very soft. It felt like a trampoline because I bounced ten feet up again. As I was falling back down, a pole appeared in the air. Naturally, I grabbed on to it to break my fall. It was five minutes before the wind cleared a little of the mist away and I was able to see what had occurred.

"To my good fortune, I'd fallen directly into the masthead of a passing square rigger. The sail had not only broken my fall, but like a rubber band, it had sent me back up again. On my way back down, I'd passed the yardarm. This is what I'd grabbed on to and was now dangling from in the fog. I could hear the voices of sailors below me, although I was quite sure they couldn't see me, as I couldn't see them. I could, however, see the crow's nest from where I was. If I could just get to it, I could climb down to the deck and I'd be safe. I began to inch my way along, hand over fist to where it was attached to the mast."

"Nobody was in the crow's nest?" Eddie asks.

"The ship was fog bound. There was nothing to see. Anyway, my arms felt ten inches longer by the time I got there, but I made it, and I was able to climb to the platform. It took me a moment to get my bearings. As I stood there, the voices became louder, and it was clear they were arguing. I heard shouts, orders given, a gunshot and something thrown into the drink. Dead silence, and then a single voice inquiring if anyone else cared to question the new command.

"At that moment, I was standing with my foot on the first rung of the ladder. I thought twice about stepping unannounced into the middle of a mutiny, and I decided to stay right where I was. At least until the fog lifted. I was there about an hour when the new captain ordered, 'Pull the anchor and loose the sails!' He'd decided to shove off despite the fog. But not half an hour out, it did begin to lift. The next time I looked down it was clear to the deck, and the captain was at the foot of the ladder, staring up.

"He was a frightful-looking fellow with black, stringy hair tied back with a dirty kerchief, and one eye permanently shut tight. 'Where'd you come from, boy?' he hollered. He tapped his bayonet sheath on the deck. 'Get down here and present yourself.'

"Well, obviously, I had no choice. I climbed down and stood before him. He glared at me with his one yellow eye. 'I asked you where you came from?' he repeated.

'I come from Tow Hill,' I answered. 'I didn't mean to disturb your ship, sir, and you have my promise I won't say anything to anyone about what you did.'

"I wasn't sure why I blurted that out, but I'd no sooner said it when I knew it was a mistake. He cocked his head and poked me with his bayonet. 'Oh, and what did I do?' he enquired.

"'Well, the gunshot, sir, and what went overboard.' I stopped myself because his face was getting snarlier as I spoke. He showed his teeth, the same horrid yellow as his eye. 'Well, you can be sure you won't,' he sneered. 'Mapface!' he hollered. At once, a squat fellow—his face a network of broken veins—stood next to him. 'Throw this boy in the hold. I'll dispose of him later. I don't like boys who drop out of the sky.'

"Mapface grabbed me by an arm. He was a short sailor, but his arm was four times the thickness of my own. He hauled me down a narrow flight of steps and along a dark passage. On either side, chains rattled and men groaned behind barred doors. Some doors had small squares cut in them. Through these, I spotted the squished faces of desperate men. 'Let us out now, and no one will be the wiser,' begged one man as we passed. Mapface ignored him. 'In there,' he growled. He stuffed me into a room with a door so low that I had to crouch to get in.

"It took several minutes for my eyes to adjust to the dark. Finally I detected half a dozen pairs of eyes around the room. Someone said something about me being just a boy. 'You a stowaway?' one of them asked. I told them, no, I'd only been beachcombing and lost my footing. They chuckled sadly at the misfortune of my stumbling into their predicament by unlucky chance. It seemed it was the cook who'd taken over the ship; he was the yellow-eyed man who was now posing as captain. He'd put something in their morning coffee to make them all fall asleep; then he locked them up while they were snoring."

"Why did he want to take over the ship?" Eddie asks.

"It wasn't clear," answers Granddad, "but I gathered from what was said that it was revenge. The men told me he was a terrible cook and they'd all been complaining. He made them eat liver and onions three times a week.

"Well, that gave me an idea. I knew I was no match for old Yellow-eye with his weapons and strong-arm tactics. I didn't say a word to anyone about my plan. When Mapface came around with our meal, sure enough, it was liver and onions. I ate it like I hadn't eaten in a week. I then called Mapface through the hole in the door and asked for a second helping. After that, I asked if I could give my compliments to the chef."

"Was it really good?" asks Eddie.

Granddad scrunches his nose. "It was awful! I could hardly swallow the first plate let alone the second. But I had to make the best of a bad situation. I knew I had no choice but to stomach it if I was to get off that ship. Well, Mapface looked very confused at my request, but he opened the door and he had me follow him to the new captain's cabin. The yellow-eyed man was surprised to see me, of course. He dabbed his mouth with his bib and looked up from his dinner of lobster and small roasted potatoes. He spoke to

Mapface, 'I thought I told you to stuff that one in the hold.' But before Mapface could answer, I stepped forward.

"'It was a special request, sir. I asked that I be allowed to tell you directly what a scrumptious meal of liver and onions you serve. I enjoyed it so much I had a second helping. If this is how you treat your prisoners, I'll gladly remain one and hope that the same meal will be served every day.' Well, you can imagine that one eye blinked like the beacon in a lighthouse. Once the captain overcame his surprise, he asked, 'You really liked it?'

"'I most certainly did. All I can say is, I wish I could take you home to my mother and you could teach her how to cook like that.' The captain stood up. 'Really? Because some of the men don't like my cooking. They say it isn't fit for pigs.'

"'Boors,' I told him. 'Only boors with no appreciation for the finer things in life would come out with a comment like that.' Well, that had the captain smiling and he immediately invited me to join him. Mapface set a chair and a place at the captain's table. I had an enjoyable meal of lobster and asparagus, and cream puffs for dessert."

"How did you get off the ship?" Eddie asks.

"Well, once I'd finished my fourth cream puff, we took our Turkish coffee to the deck. That's when the captain asked if I'd like to join his new crew; he'd make me first mate. I said I was very grateful and appreciative to be asked, but Rick would be wondering where I was. I wasn't the type to leave a buddy high and dry. He nodded, saying that he understood. Although he was disappointed, he offered to take me back to Rose Spit.

"The island was still shrouded in mist when we landed, and I made my way across the rocks. I came up behind Rick through the fog. He turned. 'What took you so long? I wanted to show you this sea urchin.' I bent down to look in the pool at what he'd found."

Eddie is laughing.

"You see, Eddie. Sometimes you have to eat the liver and onions if you want the cream puffs for dessert."

Fred drives Granddad and Grandma, along with Eddie, Jake, Mom, Peggy and Mrs. Greenshaw, to the airfield to see Granddad off. He is flying to the mainland because he is not strong enough to make the eight-hour trip by boat. Eddie had already asked if he was afraid to fly because he had never been on an airplane. Granddad said that he wasn't. Grandma, however, was wearing her favorite sweater and her string of lucky pearls around her neck.

It is raining, of course, as they gather around to say goodbye and good luck to Granddad before he boards the small plane. But nobody notices, it is so much the way of the island and a part of their lives. They each hug Granddad and give him their best wishes. Eddie has a very hard time keeping the tears from falling when it is his turn, but he doesn't want to give Granddad another reason to worry. He must let him think that he is strong and that he is able to look after things while he is gone. He must let him think he's almost a man.

"Good luck, Granddad." Eddie holds Granddad tight. His face twitches from the effort to keep back the tears.

"I love you," Granddad tells him. "Don't you worry, everything will be all right."

Eddie hopes with all his heart that it will be. But now, as Granddad squeezes back, Eddie is surprised at how really thin Granddad has become and how his arms have lost their strength.

Chapter 9

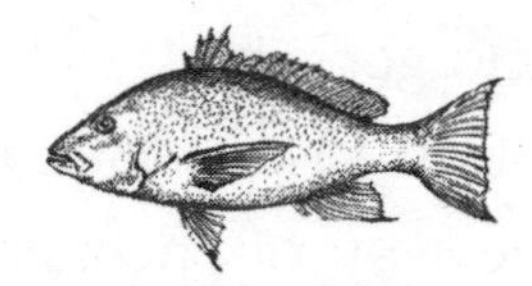

Dr. Bloom, a university professor, arrives late that afternoon. Eddie is glad their new guest is only one person, and a quiet one at that. Dr. Bloom says he has come to study the many varieties of plants on the islands. He tells Eddie there are over three hundred different types of moss alone, and there are species of ferns that date back to dinosaur times. This makes where Eddie lives very special.

Eddie doesn't feel like it's very special. He feels lost and cut off from the world with Granddad gone. He wishes the island were special enough that Granddad could get the treatments he needs right there.

Fred and Jake invite Eddie to go fishing the next morning. They walk down to the wharf together loaded down with all their gear. Fred has Eddie carry the gaff.

"That's for the whopper you're going to catch," he tells him. "I hear you've got a knack for bringing in the big fish."

Eddie shrugs. "I only hooked a whopper once and he got away."

"Yes, but you're only ten. It's just a matter of time. I didn't hook a fish big enough to pull a boat until I was nearly twenty."

"Really?" says Eddie. "It pulled your boat?"

"Oh, yes, about a mile across the bay."

"And then what happened?"

"It broke the line." Fred sets his rod and tackle box on the wharf. He steadies the boat for the boys to climb in. "That was it. He left me a mile from where we started minus a hook and lure."

"Oh," says Eddie. He was hoping for more of a story. It wasn't Fred's fault, but he knew this was going to be very different than fishing with Granddad.

While Fred fishes and sings old sailing songs, Jake and Eddie compete to see who can catch the biggest fish. By lunchtime they have pulled in eight ling cod between them, but the fish are too close in size to declare a winner. As always, every time Eddie drops his line he secretly hopes he will snag the big snapper. He scans the surface of the water as far as he can see. He remembers a story Granddad had told him a few months earlier. Granddad had been working on his new boat at the time. He was installing a brace where he could attach a belt. This was in case he was alone and caught a big fish; the belt would hold him securely so he wouldn't be pulled overboard.

"When did you last see the big snapper?" Eddie had asked him.

Granddad had straightened. He'd pressed the screwdriver to his lip as he tried to recall. "Well, now let me think about that. Not all that recently. I guess it was about a year ago. I bumped into him one day when you were at school."

"And you didn't tell me?"

"I don't tell you everything, Eddie. I don't want to bore you. Besides, it happened so fast and it was just in passing; I didn't have him on my hook or anything like that."

"What happened?" Eddie asked.

"Do you remember the storm that took the eaves trough off the cabin last December?"

Eddie nodded.

"It was that very same day. I was out fishing and you were at school. It was an unusual storm the way it blew in so fast. I could see it coming: the clouds were black and threatening in the distance, but from past experience, I thought I had a few hours before it would hit. I wasn't the only one. Many of us were caught off guard and there were a lot of fishermen on the bay.

"Well, it wasn't half an hour after I first noticed the clouds that the wind picked up. Ten minutes later it was howling, and the rain began to fall. I pulled my anchor and started the engine. By then the rain was coming down so hard, driving in from the north, it felt like small fish hooks biting into my skin. I pulled my poncho over my head. I had to squint hard through the rain to see the shore. The wind whipped the water into a real frenzy, creating two-foot swells in places. My skiff rocked dangerously, and I was afraid I was going to be swamped.

"With gales like that and judging by the speed it came in, I was pretty certain we were in for a real typhoon. I was intent on getting home. I wanted to get you home from school and secure the cabin. I couldn't get out of my mind that yellow cedar next to the southwest corner of the house. I'd been meaning to cut down. It towered right over the corner of the sitting room where Grandma liked to sit. Winds like that could bring it down.

"Anyway, it was crazy when I think about it. Everyone and everything was heading for shelter. All the boats had turned, headed toward the wharf, and the gulls had given up scavenging. They were now circling to find a place to wait out the storm. Here and there, fish rose and dolphins leapt above the whitecaps. Perhaps they were trying to catch a glimpse of what was causing the water to darken and churn. I was bouncing across the waves, the rain driving in my face, my only thought to get to the wharf as fast as I could, when it happened."

"What happened?" Eddie asked.

"The big snapper soared above the skiff and plowed right into me. We banged head-on like we were quarterbacks on opposing teams. It sent us both reeling and we landed spread-eagled on the floor of the boat; me in the bow and him in the stern. We were both momentarily stunned, the wind knocked out of us. We looked at one another and shook our heads. I could see that he was as shocked as I. On his way somewhere, probably racing to make sure his family was safe in the coming storm, he was as surprised to crash into me as I was to him. He was only in the boat for a moment, but in that instant, I was amazed at how he'd changed. He was no longer the bold young fish that had set me over the blowhole of a humpback. His bright orange hue had faded and his whiskers were gray. The responsibilities of life had left their mark.

"The wind howled and we were both suddenly aware of our duties again. As quickly as he'd appeared, the snapper sprang over the gunwale and slipped back into the dark water. He had no time to waste on me, nor did I have time to waste on him. I got behind the engine again and roared off through the storm."

"And that was it?" Eddie asked.

"And that was it. At least for the snapper." Granddad began to work on the brace again. "As you know, we lost a section of the eaves trough in that storm, and it did remind me to cut down that dead cedar the next day. That was all, though; it could have been much worse."

It's Jake who hooks the biggest fish of the day. It's late in the afternoon, and it takes nearly half an hour to land him. It's a red snapper weighing about twenty pounds. Eddie knows it's not the big snapper because it isn't missing a piece of its dorsal fin, and besides, it's far from the biggest snapper he's ever seen. Still, he congratulates Jake; it is a fine fish.

Dr. Bloom is sitting at the kitchen table chatting with Mom and Mrs. Greenshaw when Eddie arrives home. Dr. Bloom is very interested—he is more than interested—he is excited to learn about the roots and plants Jake's mom uses to make her medicines and ointments. Eddie thinks it a little strange that anyone could get so worked up about what grows on the island, but he also likes this about Dr. Bloom. He likes the way he compliments Mom on her cooking and how, since he has been on the island, he hasn't seemed to notice how much it rains.

Granddad phones after dinner. His treatments are to begin the following day. Eddie waits while Mom asks how Granddad's feeling, if he's being treated well, and if Grandma needs anything, before it is his turn to speak.

"What did you do today?" Granddad asks.

Eddie is surprised at how very small Granddad's voice sounds. He decides it must be because he is so far away. “I went fishing with Fred and Jake.” Eddie stops at that. Now that he has the phone, he can’t think of what else to say.

So he listens while Granddad tells him about his airplane ride. He tells Eddie about his drive through the city to the hospital and how nice all the people have been.

After they say goodbye, Eddie walks down to the shore carrying a bucket and his clam digging shovel. He follows the damp sand where the water meets the shore. Now and again he stops and pounds the sand with his rubber boot, looking for signs of clams. Where water squirts from a hole like a tiny geyser, he sets the point of his shovel and begins to dig straight down. He has done this often and he soon has four large clams. He walks a little farther and stomps his foot again. Ten inches away, another squirt of water rises from a hole. Eddie drops to his knees and begins to dig. He dumps a shovelful of wet sand next to his foot. The clam has dug deeper than Eddie, so he continues to dig further.

“You’ve got to be awfully fast to outrun a razor clam.”

Eddie looks up. The man in front of him bends to look in the bucket. “But you obviously are.

I see you've got four already, and they're a good size."

For a moment, Eddie just stares at the man. He knows it is impolite but he is overcome with surprise. Until a year ago his picture used to sit on the table in the sitting room.

"Hello, Eddie." The man crouches next to him. He holds out his hand for Eddie to shake.

Eddie takes his dad's hand in his own sandy wet one and shakes it. He is glad to finally know that his father is smarter than a crab, but he also wonders what took him so long to get out of the trap.

Chapter 10

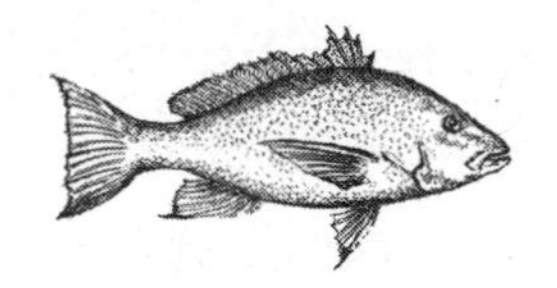

Eddie finds Dr. Bloom puttering around the kitchen, trying to find something to eat. Mom is in her room, crying. She has been there since Eddie's father arrived the night before. He is not staying in the cabin, however, but at Great-Aunt Ellen's in the village.

Eddie makes Dr. Bloom some toast and steeps a pot of spruce tea. Dr. Bloom tells him that spruce tea is his number one greatest discovery since he came to study the flora of the island. He also tells Eddie that today is his last day and he is disappointed to be leaving. Still, he's looking forward to one more trip to Naikoon Park before boarding the ferry that night. Eddie thinks he may be even sorrier to see Dr. Bloom go than

Dr. Bloom is to be leaving. He has no idea who he'll be sharing the cabin with next.

Once Dr. Bloom has left with his camera and notebook, Eddie debates whether he should go into his mother's room. He misses Grandma and he tries to think what she would do. He makes Mom some tea and toast like he had for Dr. Bloom. He then carries it to her bedroom and knocks on the door. After a minute or so, Mom opens it. She smiles when she sees the tray Eddie carries: a very lopsided, almost frightening smile because her face is puffed up like a mushroom from crying.

"Oh, Eddie," she sniffles, lifting the tray from his hands, "he doesn't deserve you and me." She sets the tray on her dresser. "Will you pass me some more Kleenex, dear?" Eddie does as she asks. He then watches as she blows her nose and dabs at a fresh flow of tears.

Eddie wanders out to the boat shed, leaving his mother to cry and eat her breakfast. He is not sure how he feels—a jumble of sadness and anger. It has kept him awake most of the night. And now that he sees Mom puffed up from crying he is so hurt and angry he could spit! Why would his dad take off and then come back like that?

He said he was going to bring them over, yet he hadn't called them in almost six months. Does he expect them to just forget about the whole past year? More than ever, he wishes Granddad was there to help sort things out. But he's not, and Eddie will have to deal with it himself.

Eddie grabs his fishing rod and tackle box and hurries down to the deserted wharf. Granddad's skiff is the only boat remaining, as the fishermen have left for the day. It is a quiet mid-morning with the exception of the eagles and their high-pitched mewing and the gulls screaming overhead. Eddie imagines they are telling him off for doing what he knows he's forbidden to do. But they don't know how badly he needs to be alone and that this is the only place he knows where he can really think.

Eddie has never driven Granddad's skiff, at least not without Granddad sitting next to him ready to take the throttle when his arm begins to ache. But he is certain he knows exactly what to do. Still, he is thankful the water is calm and there is barely a breeze.

It takes some strength to pull the starter cord. Eddie must stand tall and yank the cord as hard as he can. When the engine finally jumps to life, the throttle vibrates in his small hand. He fights with the powerful engine, but his anger seems to have built muscle and he is able to guide the boat into open water. Picking up speed, he bounces crazily across the bay. By the time he cuts the engine farther out, beyond Granddad's regular fishing spot, he is quite shaken and exhausted from the effort of simply keeping the skiff headed in the right direction.

Eddie prepares his line and casts. Less than ten minutes later he feels a tug on the line and he reels in his first fish, a five pound flounder. By noon he has caught three more. He is a little disappointed in the weather. When he'd first set out, it had been a calm and sunny day, but a heavy mist has drifted in and the sea and sky are now a dull and unhappy gray. He thinks that maybe it has turned to suit how he is feeling.

As he watches a charter boat pass Eddie hooks another fish. He can tell right away it is different than the others. This fish is big; it is strong and determined. Eddie allows it more line. He has given it what he thinks he can afford and clamped down on the drag, when all at once, the skiff starts moving. Slowly, the fish begins pulling him farther out of the bay. Eddie forgets his anger for a moment and he is at once terrified and excited. Only the one time when he was with Granddad had he hooked anything so big. He tries to remember what he is to do. He recalls Granddad telling him, "You've got the whole ocean to wear him out." So, Eddie allows the fish to continue to pull the boat.

He is concentrating so intently on the fish that he hardly notices when it begins to rain. The wind picks up. Eddie is only vaguely aware of it whistling in his ears because he is thinking about how he would like to see the fish. If he could only see it, he would know what he was up against. On the other hand, maybe it's better that he can't. If it is the big snapper, like he thinks it might be, he'd know immediately that he had no chance.

He is probably a mile from where he began when it finally occurs to Eddie that a storm is brewing. The rain is falling in enormous drops and the wind has begun to wail. For more than an hour he has not taken his eyes from the angle of the line, but now, through the curtain of mist, he sees other vessels are heading into shore. It is not possible for him to do the same because that would mean releasing his gigantic fish, which he is not about to do.

Granddad's skiff is tossed wildly in the white-caps, and Eddie becomes frightened he might be tossed right out of the boat. He suddenly remembers the braces Granddad had attached to his new boat. When the line slackens just a little, he takes advantage of the moment even though his arms ache and his shoulders have never been so sore. Holding the rod tightly in one hand, he leans hard against it to keep it secure against the skiff. He then manages to tie the rope attached to the bow around his waist and knot it to an oarlock.

Eddie remains standing, clutching the rod tightly. He is suddenly angry at the fish. At least it is in familiar surroundings, far below the surface, out of the path of the storm. Eddie has no such advantage; he must continue the fight while being tossed about with driving rain stinging his face. Well, he'll show the fish he can take it. He will show them all.

By late afternoon, the rain still has not let up and the wind continues to howl. Eddie realizes he has not passed another vessel for more than an hour. His hands are raw and he feels the

rope tied around him, cutting into his back. Tears stream down his cheeks because he is tired, cold and hurting. Still, all he wants is this fish. Then he sees—he is sure of it—the angle of the line beginning to rise. He remembers something else Granddad had said to him, "Make him think you're strong—stronger than he is. Make him think you're a very big man."

Eddie tries hard to do this. He holds fast to the rod, trying to convince the fish he is as strong as a tugboat. He straightens his back, trying to make him think he is two times the length of the skiff. If the fish wants six inches of line, Eddie gives him two. The line rises a little more, and the tension eases just a little. For the first time he thinks he may have a chance at winning, but suddenly the knot Eddie had tied comes lose and he is yanked forward. The wind is knocked out of him when he slams into the side and crashes to the bottom of the skiff. He is face down in four inches of water, yet he will not let go of the rod. He is soaked through and cold—so cold his arms and legs are numb and his teeth are chattering. Eddie tries, but he discovers he no longer has the strength in his knees to stand up, and the muscles in his shoulders are too cramped to wield the rod. He is lying on it, the weight of his body keeping it in the boat as the waves pitch the skiff back and forth.

He is not sure how long he has been there when he becomes aware that the rain has stopped falling. The rise and fall of the boat eases, and he hears a sound above the flagging wind. It is clearer now. A boat engine. And then, his name. Grabbing hold of the rod, he lifts his upper body as high as he can manage. It is Fred's boat. And in it, shouting and waving, are Fred, Jake and Eddie's dad. Fighting the wind and waves, Fred pulls alongside Granddad's skiff.

"Eddie! Are you okay?!" Eddie's dad is by his side, helping him to stand and wrestling the rod from Eddie's clenched hands. Eddie has the rod gripped so tightly that his fingers seem adhered to the fiberglass.

"It's the snapper," Eddie's voice comes out hoarse. "Don't let him go."

"Sit down here." His dad guides him to the seat in the bow. He hangs on to the rod while he struggles to remove his jacket, which he drapes over Eddie's shoulders. Eddie pulls the jacket close around him. His teeth are chattering crazily as he watches his dad take control of the rod. After testing it, he looks over at Eddie in astonishment. He begins reeling it in, a little at a time.

Eddie realizes it has been several hours since he first hooked the fish and it also must be wearing out. Certainly it is too weak to put up much of a fight against this sudden and strong new opponent. It is with ease that Eddie's father plays out what little strength the fish has left in it while Fred and Jake watch from their boat. The angle of the line is rising quickly now. Ten minutes later, Eddie gets his first glimpse of his fish. Silvery white, it is a halibut, almost the size of himself.

"Look, at that!" exclaims his father. "Eddie, how did you ever hang on to this whale?"

Jake is wildly excited. "Eddie! It's Moby Dick!"

Fred whistles. "I haven't seen one that size in some time. I'll bet he's well over one hundred and fifty pounds."

Now that he finally sees it, Eddie can hardly believe he was able to hang on to it. He only does because he is exhausted, bleeding and sore.

The fish disappears again. Eddie's dad cranks the reel, watching for it to reappear. When it does, Fred comes close enough to gaff it. His aim is good. Eddie's father lifts the fish on the gaff over the side and into the boat. The fish now lies in the four inches of water at Eddie's feet. For a moment, neither fisherman can take their eyes from Eddie's beautiful amazing fish.

His dad starts the engine. "Let's get you home, young man. Your mother is frantic. I'm afraid now both of us have some explaining to do."

Chapter 11

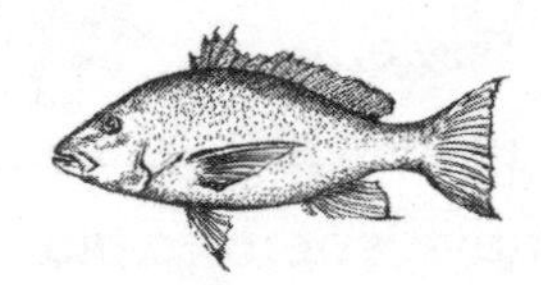

Over the next few weeks, Eddie goes fishing with his father whenever he can. Mom has stopped crying and she is now simply mad. But she has also looked after a string of tourists and without Grandma to help, she is kept so busy she really has no time to either cry or complain.

She cooks and changes sheets for the Hendersons and their two small children. She teaches four lawyers how to clean and smoke the salmon they catch on a charter boat. She tends to a sick, squawking baby while the Grossman's go whale-watching.

With so many people coming and going, Eddie realizes just how rare the quiet and studious Dr. Blooms of the world really are.

Still, in a way, he is glad when the six members of the McWilliams family arrive. Even though they are noisy and demanding, Mom continues to have no time to think of how angry she is with Dad. All six McWilliams are sleeping in Eddie's room. Mom has borrowed cots and mattresses from Peggy and Fred.

Mr. and Mrs. McWilliams are both loud and do a lot of hollering at their children. Fifteen-year-old Vince spends most of his time teasing his sister Margaret, while Margaret, who is fourteen, spends much of her time complaining to her parents about Vince. And when Jason and Janet aren't squabbling with each other, they are shouting to be heard above all the others because they are only seven and eight. Eddie has never known people who argue so much about every little thing.

The McWilliams keep Eddie busy as well. He helps serve meals and runs errands for Mom. Eddie's father offers to help, but Mom won't let him in the house. So he does what he can from a distance. He keeps the woodbox for the fireplace full and he leaves groceries on the doorstep. The first time he does this, Mom is not at all pleased.

"Where did this come from?" she asks Eddie of the bag containing bread, peanut butter and coffee left by the door.

Eddie is not sure by her tone how he should answer. But he'd seen Dad drop them off. "I think Dad left some food to help feed the McWilliams."

"Well," says his mother, "of all the nerve! I've managed this whole year without him. I hardly think I need his help now. Give them back, Eddie. Right now. Take this bag to your father."

Eddie doesn't want to give the bag of groceries back because he knows his father is only trying to help. But he also doesn't want to see the food go to waste. He carries the bag down to the wharf where his dad is preparing to go fishing.

"She doesn't want it," he tells him.

Eddie's dad shrugs. "Oh well, maybe we can use some of it for lunch. Can you come with me today?"

Eddie shakes his head. "I have to help Mom."

"Okay, maybe tomorrow then, when your guests are settled."

Eddie returns to the cabin. Vince is sitting on a log on the beach. He has broken a branch from a tree and is carving a spear. He tells Eddie he's never seen a puffin before coming to the island, and he's going to catch himself one. Eddie would like to break that spear in half before he has a chance to go after a puffin, but Vince is fifteen and he is only ten. Eddie then passes Jason and Janet who are building a sand castle. Margaret is sprawled on a blanket in the front yard, waiting for the sun to come out. Mr. and Mrs. McWilliams are making sour faces as they sip spruce tea in the sitting room.

"If you don't like the tea I could make coffee," Mom says from the kitchen.

"Oh, no," Mrs. McWilliams protests, "this is just fine." She takes another sip but her expression only gets worse.

"I'll make coffee," Mom decides. "Eddie." She pulls him to the side of the room. "Run to the market and get some coffee." She presses some money into his hand.

Eddie thinks it would have made a whole lot more sense if she'd just kept Dad's bag of groceries. But he does as she asks. As it turns out, when Eddie returns to the cabin, the coffee has been forgotten. The McWilliams family is in chaos.

As they watch through the window in the sitting room, Mom explains to Eddie that Flounder, being a dog, did not realize that Janet and Jason were building a sand castle. In his enthusiasm to chase a seagull he trampled the castle to bits. When the children began shrieking, and Vince saw what was happening, he threw his spear at Flounder. Thankfully, he missed. But thinking he was playing, Flounder retrieved the spear and began to run around with it, hoping for someone to chase him. In the process, he sprayed Margaret with sand. She was already mad because the sun had still not come out after all her waiting, and how could she return from her holidays without a tan!

Mr. and Mrs. McWilliams are, at that moment, standing in the front yard in the pouring rain, hollering out orders and directions.

"This is crazy," Mom tells Eddie, sinking into a chair. "I don't know if I'm cut out for this."

Eddie sits in the bow of the skiff, facing the open water. His father sits in the stern, guiding the boat across the bay. Once they reach Granddad's favorite spot he cuts the engine. Out of habit, Eddie attaches a piece of octopus to each of their lines.

"You're very good at that," his dad tells him.

Eddie shrugs. "I do it all the time. Granddad shakes too much."

His father sighs a little. He casts his line and lets the spool unwind to the proper depth. "I'm afraid your granddad is not very well, Eddie."

Eddie is also concentrating on letting his line out but he turns at this. "Have you seen him?"

His dad nods. "I met him at the airport. I helped him and Mom get settled in the hospital."

"Did he know you were coming home?"

"Yes, he did."

"He didn't tell me."

"No, I don't think he wanted to upset you and your mother before I got here. Besides, it's up to me to explain myself, not him."

Eddie feels a tug on the line. A fish is testing. It tugs a little harder, but it doesn't bite.

"Doesn't look like he went for it."

Eddie lifts the rod. There is no resistance. "No."

Propping his fishing rod between his legs, Eddie's father opens the thermos and pours a cup of tea. "Want some?"

Eddie shakes his head.

Dad sips his tea and takes hold of the rod

again. “Did Granddad ever tell you about the big snapper?”

Eddie nods.

“About how he pulled him all the way to Alcatraz?”

Eddie laughs a little. “Yeah, he did.”

“Hmm. How about the way he got on Trotter’s good side so he’d let him fish down at the river?”

“Uh-huh.”

Dad chuckles. “Well, here’s one he wouldn’t have told you because it happened to me. It was about three years ago.”

“You’re going to tell me a story?”

“Well, I’m going to try. Don’t expect anything as good as you’d hear from your Granddad, though. Anyway, you were just a little guy at home with your mom and Grandma at the time. I was out fishing with your granddad on a day much like today. We were fishing this very same spot, as a matter of fact, because Dad said it’s where the biggest fish are found. ‘You may not catch as many,’ he told me, ‘but what you catch is worthwhile.’

“Well, we must have been sitting here for two hours when I got frustrated. I was an impatient and headstrong fellow in those days. When three hours passed without a single strike, I decided if those big fish weren't going to come to us, I'd scare them up myself. So, I set my rod aside and pulled on my scuba gear. Dad warned me it was a mistake, but I didn't listen. I dove into the water to find the biggest fish."

"Really?" says Eddie. "How were you going to catch them?"

"I hadn't really thought of that. Anyway, I was strong and a good swimmer. I dove down through the murk, steering clear of a sawfish and his lethal snout. I swam around a giant jellyfish, but then I almost got tangled in the tentacles of a vampire squid. I dove deeper, passing all shapes and sizes of sea creatures. I came upon an old Buick balanced on a rock outcrop, and on the very bottom, the rotting remains of a fancy yacht.

"I made my way across the ocean floor. The eyes of the bottom fish gazed up at me, watching me from where they lay buried in the sand. There were big ones, but they were still not big enough for me. I wanted the biggest one. I wanted to be the greatest fisherman on the wharf. Then suddenly, through the kelp forest, a gleam caught my eye. I weaved between the kelp stalks toward the source of the light. What I came upon was the biggest oyster I'd ever seen in my life. It was big enough for a man to stand up in. But even more amazing, right in the center of the soft pink flesh was a pearl as white as whalebone and the size of a balloon.

"Well, you can imagine, after coming upon that I forgot about the fish. I would take that pearl and I would be truly famous. I swam to the oyster to lift it out. I had my arms around it—it was heavy and it did not easily budge. So I stood right inside the oyster, trampling the soft flesh, and rocked it back and forth. But instead of coming loose, to my horror, the oyster shut tight."

"Could you see anything?" Eddie asks.

"Very little. The pearl was luminous and gave off a little light, but it was mostly dark. Well, now I forgot about the pearl and I became intent on getting out. I pushed and prodded. I hammered from within, but that oyster shell wouldn't budge. I had no stick to wedge it open, or a knife to cut the foot. After hours of banging and clawing at the shell, I finally sank to the gooey bottom and tried to think of what to do next. I did discover the oyster had trapped a little air, so I was able to take off my heavy tanks.

"Hours passed, and I tried many more times. Still, that oyster wouldn't open. I became very hungry. With nothing else to eat, I picked off bits of oyster flesh. Days passed and that oyster showed no signs of opening. By then I'd eaten quite a bit of it, and I began to wonder what I'd do when there was nothing left.

"I was sleeping on the cold hard shell when a change in light woke me. I was also drowning. The shell had come open and the oyster was dead. I'd eaten too much. I quickly pulled on my scuba gear and glanced around at what was left of the oyster. Strips of shredded gray flesh hung from the inside of the shell. And the pearl—the pearl had lost its shine and was dull and gray as well. I blinked. The light, even deep beneath the ocean, was strong compared to what it had been inside the shell. Slowly, I stood up. My legs and joints were stiff from being cramped up for so long. I left the pearl and headed for the surface.

"Swimming was difficult, as I had lost a lot of strength. It was all I could do to move ten feet up, and I'd have to rest before I could move on. I had made only a little progress when I got caught in the upsweep of a current. The cooler flow of water carried me hundreds of feet with little effort. I don't know how I would have made it otherwise.

"Your granddad was alone in the boat when I surfaced. 'There you are,' he said when he saw me. 'I've been waiting for you.'

"They were the most welcoming words, and Dad in his skiff was the most comforting sight I'd ever seen. He leaned over the edge and helped me climb back in."

When his dad says nothing more, Eddie realizes the story is over. "Is that why you left?" he asks. "Because you saw a pearl?"

Eddie's father thinks about this. "No, I left because I saw something different. I came back because I'd left a pearl behind."

Eddie adjusts his cap and concentrates hard on his line. "Why did you stay?" he asks.

It is the first time he has come out and asked this question. It frightens him to ask it now, because he's not sure he wants to hear the answer.

"When I first went to the mainland," Dad begins, "I couldn't believe how much there was to see and do. There were stores and restaurants and theaters. There were huge arenas to watch concerts and sports. I thought if I made enough money I could bring you and your mother over, and we would have a much more exciting life."

"Why didn't you?"

"Because, six months later, even working two jobs, I could barely afford the little apartment where I was living. I knew it was no place for you or your mom. And despite all the people I'd met, none of them were really part of my life. I had met no Freds to help me carry heavy loads, or Mrs. Greenshaws to give me medicine when I got sick. And no matter how long I worked at that car wash or drove that taxicab, I would never have a chance to battle a great fish. After that I realized what I'd done and I was ashamed to come back."

Eddie doesn't answer for a while. Finally he says, "You shouldn't be ashamed. You made us sad, but you did come back."

Dad smiles and ruffles the hair on Eddie's head.

They catch twelve salmon between them. Once the skiff is moored, Eddie walks down the path next to his father. He helps Eddie store the rods and tackle in the shed. He then carries the baskets of fish to the kitchen door. After setting them down, he says goodbye to Eddie and starts across the yard. Suddenly the door is opened by Eddie's mother.

"Here," Eddie says, lifting a basket of fish. "Dad and I caught enough to feed the McWilliams." Eddie holds his breath, hoping she won't refuse it, especially with Dad watching.

But Mom doesn't even seem to think about it when she accepts the fish. "Thank you," she whispers to Eddie. She then looks at Eddie's father. Eddie hopes she will say it again, loud enough for him to hear this time. She does speak louder but what she says is not what either of them expects.

"Joe," Mom's voice is not mad or upset. It is soft with worry. "Your father is coming home tomorrow—earlier than expected. They say further treatments won't do much good."

Chapter 12

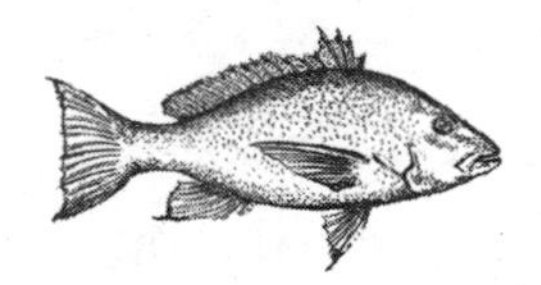

Through the sitting room window, Eddie watches his mother and father step from the wharf into Granddad's skiff. Dad starts the engine. He skillfully steers the boat through the fishing traffic until it disappears into the mist. Eddie returns to Granddad's bedroom and sits next to the bed where his grandfather lies sleeping. He has been sleeping almost constantly since he arrived home three days before.

Mom says she will not take in any more tourists until Granddad is feeling better, and the cabin is strangely quiet. Eddie whistles a little song to himself simply to hear some noise. He arranges the fishing magazines on the table next to Granddad's bed.

Someone knocks four times on the kitchen door. Eddie recognizes the knock as Jake's, and he runs down the hall to open the door. Jake stands next to the old bike with the big wooden wagon attached.

"Can you go riding yet?"

Eddie shakes his head. "I can't. I'm minding Granddad. Mom and Dad have gone fishing."

"Oh." Jake is clearly disappointed. "It's getting boring riding around by myself."

"I should be able to soon," Eddie tells him. "He can't sleep forever. I just want to hear him talk."

Jake nods. He swings a leg over the seat and slowly sets off down the path. When Eddie returns to Granddad's room, this time his grandfather's old gray eyes are open.

"Granddad!" Eddie sits next to him. "I've been waiting for you to wake up."

Granddad smiles a little, although it doesn't come as easily as Eddie remembers. It doesn't stay on his face long either. When he shifts positions, he grimaces with pain. Not sure what else to do, Eddie offers him a sip of water from a cup through a bent straw. He is placing the straw between his grandfather's dry lips, when he hears Grandma return from shopping in the village. She sets down the groceries before she appears in the doorway. Eddie leaves her to help Granddad to the bathroom, give him the medicine he's supposed to take and try and get him comfortable again.

This has been the routine of the last three days. By the time Grandma leaves the room and Eddie peeks in, Granddad is always sleeping again.

Eddie is in his own bedroom, turning over a plastic toy left behind by one of the McWilliams, or perhaps it was a Backhouse, when Grandma sticks her head in the doorway an hour later. "Your Granddad would like to see you, Eddie."

Eddie can hardly believe what he's heard. Dropping the toy, he runs across the hall to his grandfather's room. Granddad is sitting up in bed, at least as high as he can, supported by a mound of pillows. He smiles when he sees Eddie return. Eddie sits next to him and takes his hand. He is surprised at how thin it is.

"How are you, Eddie?" Granddad's voice is coarse, barely a whisper. It does not sound anything like it should.

Eddie answers that he is fine.

"What have you been up to?"

Eddie shrugs. "Hanging around with Jake. Fishing with Dad and helping Mom."

Granddad smiles again.

"Can you tell me about your trip to the mainland now?"

For many seconds Granddad does not answer, and it seems to Eddie that he is searching. At first Eddie thinks it is for the right words. But when Granddad's face tightens and the furrows in his forehead deepen, Eddie understands that he is searching for some memory of going there at all.

"It's okay, Granddad," Eddie tells him. "You can tell me another time."

Eddie pats Granddad's hand. He is trying to be reassuring, but really he wants to cry. He is suddenly remembering Mrs. Greenshaw's words: "As long as he's telling stories there's nothing to worry about. When those stop, that's when we'll get concerned."

It takes a great deal of effort for Eddie to stop the tears from flowing; he looks down at the floor, bites his lip and squeezes his eyes tight. When he looks up again, he sees the tears welling up in Granddad's own eyes. His heart aches for his old grandfather.

"Granddad." Eddie pulls his chair closer. "I have something to tell you. It happened while you were away."

Eddie is nervous. He is not sure how to tell a story, especially to Granddad, but it's the only thing he can think of doing.

"We caught the big snapper."

Granddad's expression brightens, and suddenly his eyes are shining through the tears. Eddie dabs his grandfather's eyes with a Kleenex.

"It was while you were on the mainland," he continues. "On a day very much like today. Me and Jake were out with Dad in the skiff. We were anchored right in your very own favorite fishing spot."

The twinkle in Granddad's eyes encourages Eddie to go on.

"Anyway, we'd caught five or six rock cod altogether. Then Dad got another strike. He was lying in the stern, half asleep, with his hat pulled over his face. He was feeling pretty good since he'd got his knack for fishing back. Jake noticed it first. 'Hey, Joe, heads up!' he said to Dad. It wasn't much of a bite. It didn't jerk Dad forward or anything, so we didn't think the fish could be very big. But when Dad started reeling it in, he could tell it wasn't all that small. He said it was a hefty one. It was the weight of the fish that told him that because it wasn't putting up much of a fight. It almost seemed like it took it a while to realize it had even been caught.

"When it did finally start fighting, the boat turned, and it began pulling us out to sea. But it was not very hard and it was not fast. We had barely left the bay when suddenly it was not pulling us at all. Dad was able to bring it in easily after that, a few feet at a time. It was about thirty minutes later that we got our first glimpse of Dad's fish. 'A snapper,' we all said. 'And a big one,' added Jake.

"Dad and I looked at each other. Neither of us believed it could be your big snapper and we shook our heads. Your snapper would have pulled us to Alaska and back in that time.

"Dad told us to get the gaff. Jake grabbed it and stood in the boat, waiting to hand it to Dad, when the snapper surfaced again. But when it did, it was already so worn out that Dad waved the gaff away. 'No need for that. He's all played out.' Dad raised the line as high as he could and all three of us grabbed hold of the fish and hauled him into the boat."

Granddad is trying to say something. Eddie leans closer so he can hear. He sits back again.

"We didn't know it right away, but yeah, it was your snapper. He was lying on the bottom of the boat, puffing at the gills. He was as pale as a pumpkin and his skin hung off in places like rags. That's how Dad described him. He said he was like a salmon come home to spawn. 'He's an old guy too,' he said, 'maybe sixty, seventy years old. Huh, imagine getting caught after all those years.'

"Dad didn't say anything else. He just started the engine and headed for the wharf. He didn't seem all that proud of the snapper he'd caught, maybe because it hadn't been much of a fight. Me and Jake didn't say anything either. We just looked at the snapper where he lay on the floor of the skiff. His head rested in the dent that you got in the boat when you landed on the rocks at Alcatraz.

"Then, somehow, I just knew it was him. I saw where his fin had been sliced by your prop. It hadn't been obvious at first because all of his fins were tattered. His whiskers were gray and his eye was hazy, but by the way he looked at me, I could tell that at one time it had burned black and bright. Like you said it did.

"When we reached the wharf, the other fishermen crowded around. They slapped Dad on the back and they told him it was 'a hell of a catch.' 'That fellow's an old one,' someone said, 'must be fifty, sixty years old! You did good, Joe!' We moored the boat and between the three of us, we carried the snapper to the cabin and laid it on the filleting table outside the shed. Jake went home. Dad patted the side of the snapper. 'I'll be right back with the knife,' he said quietly.

"We had so many guests while you were away, Granddad. We had the six McWilliams and the Backhouses, and the Northorpes came back. Mr. McWilliams walked by as I was standing next to the table. He looked at the big snapper. To grab his interest I said, 'He's sixty years old.' But I could tell he wasn't impressed. 'Hmm,' he said, 'is that so? Well the kids are clamoring for supper, so you might tell your mother to get him on the barbecue as soon as she can.'

"Becky Northorpe wandered by next. 'Take a look at this snapper,' I told her. 'He's a real old one.' But Becky barely glanced at the snapper before she curled her lip and said, 'Are we having fish again? Yuck, I can't stand the slimy things.'

"The snapper struggled in the air. While I waited for Dad to come back, I poured a bucket of water over him so he wouldn't suffer. The Northorpes, the Backhouses and the McWilliams were gathering at the picnic table. The moms and dads tied bibs around their children's necks. They tied napkins around their own necks and sat at the table. After a while they became impatient; they wanted to eat their supper. Clutching their forks and knives, they banged them on the table, yelling, 'We're hungry!' and 'Where's our chow?'

"Dad came to the door of the kitchen carrying a big knife. I looked at him, then over at the table where people were bellowing for their supper. They had no appreciation of what they were about to eat. They didn't care that the snapper had stayed alive for sixty years. They didn't know that he'd tricked you and pulled you all the way to Alcatraz. They had no idea how hard he'd worked to keep his own children out of the fishermen's nets. They didn't deserve him. I ran into the boat shed and grabbed my bike. I hooked up the wagon that me and Jake had rescued from the dump. I lifted the big snapper from the filleting table, loaded him into the wagon and took off. I roared down the path before anyone realized what I had done.

"When they did, the McWilliams and the Northorpes and the Backhouses jumped from the table and came after me. Still wearing their bibs and waving their utensils in the air, they shrieked and hollered all the way down the path. But they couldn't catch me. Vince fell flat on his face when he tripped over a rock, and Becky got slapped in the face by a branch.

"But I didn't stop. I bumped onto the wharf and rode across the deck. The wheels of the old wagon clattered on the rough boards as I made my way to the end. I braked hard. The wagon with its heavy load ran into my leg and almost sent me flying overboard, but I kept my balance. I bent down, wrapped my arms around the big snapper, and with more strength than I ever knew I had, I picked him up and dropped him over the side of the wharf. I watched as he slipped between the fishing boats and disappeared beneath the water. The crowd caught up to me, but it was too late. The big snapper was gone.

"You fool!' Mr. Northorpe bawled at me.

"Now what are we going to eat?!' one of the Backhouse twins screeched.

"Even the seagulls that had followed the wagon as I rode down the path screamed at me. They'd been hoping for their own taste of the big snapper.

"But I didn't pay attention to any of them. I didn't take my eyes from the waves until half a mile out I thought I saw a pale orange head appear. I waved an arm over my head, and after that he was gone. I started back down the wharf, pushing my bike with the empty wagon attached.

"The Northorpes, the McWilliams and the Backhouses grumbled and complained. They shook their fists at me but there was nothing more they could do. They ripped off their bibs and shuffled behind me across the wharf. Where the wharf met the path, I ran into Dad. He was still holding the big knife but he had a smile on his face. 'Here Eddie,' he said, pulling my bike onto the path, 'let me help you with that.'"

Except for the soft sound of breathing, Granddad's room is suddenly quiet. Eddie leans forward again. "That's the end of my story, Granddad. Did you like it?"

Granddad does not say anything, and Eddie becomes worried because his eyes have become as misty as the island where they live. But then he smiles a little, and Eddie knows it is not because he is sad.

"Dad says he won't be back," he tells his grandfather. "Dad says that's the last we'll see of the big snapper."

"Yes," Granddad whispers, nodding his head. He squeezes Eddie's hand. "And that is as it should be."

Katherine Holubitsky's first novel, *Alone at Ninety Foot* (Orca), won the CLA Book of the Year for Young Adults and the IODE Violet Downey Book Award. Since then, she has written *Last Summer in Agatha* (which won the R. Ross Annett Alberta Book Award), *The Hippie House* and *The Mountain that Walked*, all published by Orca. *The Hippie House* was also nominated for the CLA Book of the Year Award and the Arthur Ellis Crime Writers Award. Katherine lives in Edmonton, Alberta.

Other books by Katherine Holubitsky

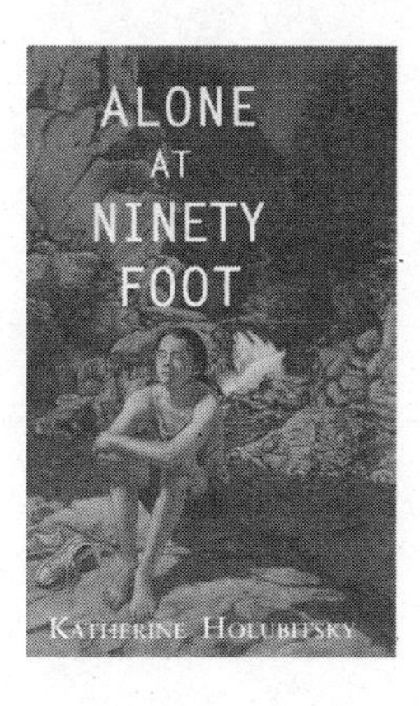

Alone at Ninety Foot
1-55143-204-8 PB

CNIB Tiny Torgi Audio Award Nominee 2001

PNLA Young Readers Choice Award nominee 2002

IODE Violet Downey Book Award

CLA Book of the Year for Young Adults Award

OAC Ruth Schwartz Children's Book Award nominee

ALA/YALSA Best Books for Young Adults 2000

OLA Red Maple Award nominee 1999

ALA Quick Pick nominee

ABA Pick of the Lists

NY Public Library Books for the Teen Age

Manitoba Young Readers Choice Award nominee 2001

CCBC Our Choice Starred selection

CBC This Morning Book Panel selection

Teacher Librarian Magazine Best Books
for Young Adults selection

Other books by Katherine Holubitsky

The Hippie House
1-55143-316-8 HC

Starred Our Choice 2005

CLA Young Adult Canadian Book Award nominee 2005

Manitoba Young Readers' Choice Award nominee 2006

Arthus Ellis Award nominee 2005

Resource Links' Year's Best 2004